# HUCK AND HER TIME MACHINE

'It's a Time Machine,' shrieked Huck. 'It just came to me in a flash – I suddenly knew.'

Huck's twin brother Barty had brought the extraordinary contraption home from the waste tip and the only place they could keep it safe from their infuriating elder brothers and sister was their mother's bedroom.

Huck's family was a trial to her. Barty spent his time drawing complicated diagrams of electronic devices which never worked. Polly rallied her friends to take up useless causes; at the moment they were picketing the prison where the prisoners were on hunger strike, but whether it was to stop food getting in or the prisoners getting out no one was quite sure. Jake was a tease and a bully, and Edward thought only about cricket and cricket scores – when he wasn't digging up history. How could Huck write beautiful poetry, let alone win the Nobel prize for literature in such an atmosphere?

But now she had a Time Machine. Could she send her family back in time and return them again more liveable with?

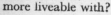

GILLIAN AVERY

# HUCK AND HER TIME MACHINE

FONTANA · LIONS

First published 1977 by William Collins Sons & Co Ltd
First published in Fontana Lions 1978
by William Collins Sons & Co Ltd
14 St James's Place, London SW1

© Gillian Avery 1977

Printed in Great Britain
by William Collins Sons & Co Ltd, Glasgow

For Shenka
who was so encouraging

# I

THE rods pointed up at the grey skies. Barty kicked at them morosely, stared down, and then crouched on the cindery track and peered at them. There was no one to see him. The huge marshy tracts of the Meadow stretched emptily all round him, fringed by willow trees and occupied only on this cold late afternoon of a cold spring day by ponies and cattle who grazed the scanty grass in the distance. Beyond them again, poplars marked where the river wound in great S-bends. In any case, he had climbed over the gate into the rubbish tip – the end that had been filled in and was waiting to be re-sown with grass – and here he rarely saw anybody, except the occasional scavenger like himself.

The Meadow had always played a great part in the lives of the Huxtables. In the summer they bathed in the river like all the other children who lived near. They flew kites there, begged rides on the ponies, raced their bikes up and down the hummocks, slid on the ice that covered the flooded ground in the winter. And they took a great interest in the rubbish. There were treasures to be had in the ground where the earth had been recently tipped. In the summer it was a jungle of plants that had come from gardens and had been flung out with the rubbish. You could gather armfuls of evening primroses and Michael-mas daisies and marigolds, and nobody cared. If you poked between them and scratched away a little earth you came across old pram frames, shoes and saucepans, gloves and bedsprings, and of course bottles and broken china by the ton.

Barty had so often hunted rubbish there that he knew exactly what he might expect to find. His connoisseur's eye would drift over the miscellaneous debris that littered the undulating surface, and would pause only when there was something that was different. And this was certainly different, even though not much of it emerged above the ground. It looked as though it was part of a highly complex and beautifully constructed piece of machinery – not one of the usual bits of bed frame or old bicycle – and that in itself appealed to his engineer's mind. He could see a dial, the beginnings of an elaborate structure of delicate rods, and what might once have been a saddle. He started scrabbling in the loose earth.

Half an hour later he was still there. The object now stuck out of the shallow pit that he had scratched away round it. He had forgotten the north wind that was hurtling over the Meadow, numbing his face and making his eyes water, and his mood of gloomy resentment about the way the Easter holidays had started. All his mind now was given to the problem of how to extract his treasure from the earth without damaging it. Anybody else might have wrenched it out, but Barty had infinite patience where machinery was concerned. He wanted it intact. As a matter of fact, it seemed surprisingly tough. It was caked in earth, of course, but when he poked this away the metal underneath hadn't rusted or corroded. But the more of it that was disclosed, the more puzzled he was about what it could possibly have been. It looked as if it could have been some sort of vehicle, because the shape of a saddle was unmistakable, even though it had lost its leather covering. And there were handlebars too. But these were rigid and immovable; at no time, it seemed, could they ever have been used to steer, only to hold on to. Nor was there any trace of wheels, or indeed any place for them in the design. Holding the handlebars and the saddle, he pulled, experimentally. It felt amazingly light in his hands, and it came away from the loose earth quite easily.

Barty dusted his grimy hands on his jeans and stared at it. The next thing was to get it home and clean it up a bit. Looking round, he saw the four wheels of an old pram a few yards off. Tenderly he lifted his machine on to this, and started on the journey home.

Simon Street is a good twenty minutes' walk from the Meadow at the best of times, and if you are bent double over a pram chassis which you are trying to steer over the pavement of busy streets, it takes at least twice as long. All Barty's mood of smouldering discontent had returned by the time he finally straightened himself up outside the battered, blistered door of the house in Simon Street. When he had left, there had been no one there, now his brothers and sisters had taken it over. He could tell that without going in. For one thing, the whole building was vibrating, swaying, to the sound of Jake's drums from the bedroom where he was accompanying a tape. There had been a time when the neighbours complained about it, but long ago it had been realized that this was useless, and those who really wished for a quiet life moved from the Huxtables' neighbourhood. The bookroom on one side of the front door was occupied by Edward; he could see him through the window sprawled there among books and papers. And in the sitting-room on the other side Polly and Huck were arguing furiously; even though he couldn't hear their voices he could see their angry faces, their gestures. As Barty pushed open the door there was a sudden silence – the tape and the drums had simultaneously come to an end – and then the sound of crashing china. Huck came out from the sitting-room door.

'I've just thrown a mug at Polly,' she remarked. 'I had

9

to. What on earth's that?'

She was Barty's twin, though they were as different in appearance as they were by nature: Barty; fair, neat, precise; Huck; swarthy, flamboyant and tempestuous. Once her name had been Hannah. It was Hannah until she was five. Then she had announced that she loathed the name, that she refused to have it any more, that she was going to kill it. She had produced a matchbox which she said was its coffin. The matchbox had been buried in the trampled patch of bare earth at the back of the house (it was known as 'the garden' though nobody would have recognized it as such). There had been a headstone, long since disappeared, which said, 'Here lies Hannah. Dead and berried for ever. Good riddens!' The problem had then been what to call herself, because her parents had given her only the one name, having run out of ideas by the time of their fifth child. Huck did not care; she could be called plain Huxtable, she said; Huck for short. And Huck she had been, so securely that very few people could even remember there once had been another name. She stood on the doorstep now, staring at the object that Barty was lifting off the pram.

'Are you going to bring it indoors?'

Barty hesitated. Certainly he was going to bring it in, but he had not the least idea where he was going to put it. That was the trouble in this house, it was impossible to have any privacy. He would not dream of taking anything he really cared about into the bedroom that he shared with Jake, who would only mock and tease, and where else was there that was not trampled over by the family and their friends?

'It can go in Mother's room. She won't be back for a week.'

'But what is it, anyway? Have you really gone and made a machine for once instead of just drawing them?'

Irritatingly she watched him as he struggled upstairs with it. It wasn't heavy, it was just awkward to carry, this box-like shape with its maze of rods. She could have offered to help him – not that he would have allowed her to touch it, but at least she could have offered instead of just standing there asking idiotic questions.

'No, of course you didn't make it,' she said, coming in behind him as he put it down on the rug by the bed. She stooped and peered at it short-sightedly through her glasses. 'That's proper machinery. And all dirty. I suppose you got it from the Meadow.'

'And what's wrong with that?'

'I didn't say there was, did I! What a weird contraption, I don't see what anybody could have used it for – I mean, there aren't any parts that could move, it's all rods and wires stuck together.'

In the next room – Jake's and Barty's – there were restless movements. Huck could recognize what these meant.

'Quick, let's get out before he comes and starts interfering. Pretend to be doing something else.'

So when Jake loafed out of the bedroom a few minutes later, it was to find Huck and Barty sitting on the stairs, Huck gabbling out of a book that she held on her knees, Barty staring gloomily over her head.

'Shut up,' said Huck without looking up. 'Go away, leave us alone.'

'I haven't started yet.' Jake came down the stairs and peered over her shoulder. 'What are you doing? Reading to him?'

'I'm trying to educate him. You know how he won't read anything that isn't facts. Don't listen to him, Barty; listen to me.'

'What are you educating him with? Dante? Shakespeare? Homer? Oh, I see, just H. G. Wells.'

'He likes inventions and things,' said Huck crossly, 'so I thought he might like *The Time Machine*. And I'd just got him to listen and *you* had to barge in.'

'And do you enjoy it?' Jake asked Barty. 'A casual observer might think otherwise.'

'It's all right, I suppose,' said Barty moodily. Huck had been reading to him out of this book for weeks now, on and off. It seemed to be a huge wad of words which just went on and on and told him nothing.

'And what are the bits that are most all right? – to imitate your eloquence?'

Barty looked blank. The fact was, he had not the remotest idea what the book was about.

'I don't believe you've ever listened to a word,' Huck shouted at him accusingly. 'All this time I've wasted, and me getting sore throats from reading!'

'I remember about him trying the screws and oiling the rods,' said Barty defensively.

'Oil and screws! Who wants to hear about those!'

'Barty does, evidently. He's for facts, you're for fancy – pity somebody doesn't bang your heads together and try and mix you up a bit. I could make a start by banging your heads, anyway.' Jake lunged towards them.

'Stop it,' shrilled Huck, standing up and beating at him with the book. 'Polly, Edward, come and help. Jake's bullying.'

Of course nobody came. But Jake, who, with his long arms and superior strength, might have managed to carry out his threat, was interrupted by thunderous knocking on the front door. Huck threw down her book and charged.

'I bet that's Lucy Soper, and I'm going to bash her back teeth in this time. And I'm not going to help her pick them up, either.'

The knocking had brought Polly to the sitting-room

door, and in the bookroom the sound of creaking springs showed that even Edward had been roused. Huck wrenched at the door handle. 'You've got it coming to you, Lucy Soper, so you watch out!' she shouted. 'Oh!' Her voice changed as she saw the visitor.

There was no child of Huck's size on the doorstep, but a Goliath from the city constabulary. He looked past Huck to Edward, who was now standing in the hall, uneasily clutching his book. Edward after all was the eldest of the Huxtables though he rarely had much idea of what his brothers and sisters were doing. The policeman jerked his finger at Huck. 'In trouble again. She's laid out another kid in the gutter, that's what she's been doing. Someone in the street saw it happen, came and told me.'

'Was it Lucy Soper?' said Polly severely to Huck.

'She sent my marble down the drain. She said it was an accident, but of course it wasn't. Then she sort of ran against my head and it made her fall down.'

'Knocked out the other kid with her head. You'd think she was a prize bull. Where's your mum?' said the policeman wearily.

'She's gone away,' said Barty dejectedly. 'There was a note on the kitchen table when we got back from school, saying "Gone to America. Tea in the oven, money in the soup tureen. Back for Easter."' All his mood of desolation returned as he remembered how he had rushed in and had found it. Of course she did often leave them, but not usually with so little warning, nor on the very first day of the holidays.

'Leaving the police to act as nursemaids and pick up the bits, I suppose. *As* usual. And school holidays just starting. What's she after this time?' asked the policeman, with the air of one who had suffered much at her hands.

'Something about equality or freedom,' said Barty vaguely. 'I'm not sure who for. It might be Africans. Or women, or people in prison, or students.'

'It's no good asking him,' said Huck contemptuously. 'He's only interested in his old machines and inventions.'

'Whereas you,' said Jake sweetly, 'are only interested in inventing stories. But what is Mother after this time, does anybody know?'

'She may have told us,' said Edward perplexed, 'though I don't immediately recall it.' He was pulling at his nose. Already long, it would, it seemed, grow to trunk-like size before the end of his life by his habit of tugging at it when he was confronted by a problem. 'We could probably find out,' he added helpfully.

'The fact that our Edward remembers that we *were* told,' said Jake, 'shows what a dead time of year it is for cricket-watching. If it had been winter he would have been following the cricket news from Australia; if it was summer he would have been watching it here. But all he can do now is . . .'

'And all you can do is talk,' said the policeman. 'Well, I suppose it doesn't matter what she's doing, the fact is, she's gone.'

'It's her Globe Freedom Movement,' said Polly fiercely. 'And it matters very much indeed.'

'She's got freedom for herself all right. If it wasn't that she was Mrs Huxtable and had such a way with her, you lot would have been took in care years ago instead of roaming the streets like young savages.'

Polly's voice rang down Simon Street. 'Mother has a perfect right to go where she likes, when she likes. That's what Globe Freedom's about, in case you didn't know. Women have a right to be free, so have their children.'

'Chip off the old block, isn't she,' said the policeman indifferently. 'You save your breath, my girl. We've heard it all many a time before from your mum. And give us that money while I'm here; I suppose she's left it for the police station to be bank, like the usual.'

It was Barty who went to the kitchen and came back with a torn and dirty envelope. 'I expect it's in here.'

'It is, and a letter too. You'd better look at that while I count the notes and give you a receipt. It may be something important.'

'If it is then that is precisely why Mother abandoned it.' Jake, who had come lounging down the passage, was now propped against the door frame, indolently scanning the street. 'If you see what I mean.'

'I can see that your hair needs cutting. But I never knew the time when it didn't.'

Jake ran his fingers through the tangled mass of corkscrew curls that stood like a bush round his head. 'They say something of the sort every day at school. It's like the dripping of a tap, one ceases to notice it after a time. Well, Poll, was it an important letter?'

'Just the Town Hall, asking Mother for an immediate reply to something or other.'

'An immediate answer – from *Mother*. What a hope,' said Jake idly. 'It must be some new chap asking.'

The policeman reached past him to Edward. 'You'd better take charge of this receipt, you being the eldest – though more often you act like a babe unborn. Most families as old as you lot wouldn't need anybody to keep an eye on them. It's lucky we've got a superintendent who's soft on your mum and all you, and willing to act as nursemaid and father and mother and social security and the whole outfit. Soft on the younger generation altogether he is, a great deal too soft – likes to forget he's a copper most of the time. I don't know what he's doing in the force at all. You'll be down from time to time to show yourselves and collect the necessary, same as usual, I take it? And for pity's sake try to stop your sister going for people or she'll be in proper trouble one of these days, I'm giving you fair warning.'

The door slammed shut and they could hear the heavy tread clacking away over the pavement. Jake pulled it open and called across the street in fluting tones. 'That is the end of today's little Huxtable drama. You can now let your lace curtains drop and return to your television sets. Well, Huck, you *are* a little object! Edward, look at your baby sister.' He snapped on the light in the book-room. Edward, who had retreated there some minutes ago, looked up from the armchair where he was sprawled and blinked in the sudden glare of the unshaded bulb.

'Somebody saw Huck clobbering Lucy Soper and complained,' said Polly, 'as you might have gathered if you took the slightest interest in the world about you. I must say it's a bit hard on the Sopers. They're always taking pity on Huck and having her round, and what does she do but bash up Lucy.'

Edward, with creased forehead, gazed at Huck. 'She looks rather muddy,' he said vaguely.

Huck's legs were encrusted with dirt – what you could see of them below the Afghan coat that she was clutch-ing round herself. (She picked her clothes from the local jumble sales with any money she could scrounge.) She peered down at them complacently. 'We were kneeling in the gutter. It's good, isn't it? Dirt is history. People die and turn to dust and plants grow out of their corpses and they die and turn to earth and slime and . . .'

'And you smear the mud all over you and Lucy Soper,' said Jake.

'That's right. So it might be Shakespeare or someone that I've got on my knees.'

'And Dickens in between your toes and Hitler behind your ears.'

'Hitler was *German*,' said Huck with crushing force. 'There were some Americans today.' Her face took on the dreamy look that Barty knew well. 'They were standing in the High and staring at one of the colleges – you know, the one that is being all washed and repaired. And there was a woman with her hair dyed bright purple. And she said, "Think of all that history up there. If that tower could write it would be a history book in itself." So I said . . .'

'Look at my neck, you said. Or the bath after I've been in it.'

'I didn't!' screeched Huck, trying vainly to stamp on Jake's toes. 'I said, you don't understand about history. They're washing all the history off those stones. If you want real history, I said, you ought to go to a rubbish dump. My brother Edward goes down to St Botolph's to dig up stones from an old church. I don't know why he bothers. I could show him history without having to dig. I could show you too, I said to her. You come to our house. It's full of history, though you mightn't think so to look at it.'

'Crumbs,' suggested Jake, 'cobwebs, stains on the ceiling.'

But Huck was so carried away by her narrative that she paid no attention. 'Letters and pictures and photographs. My diaries, Grandpa's school cap – that's history, I said, not kings and queens and dates and buildings . . .'

'You didn't say anything of the sort,' said Polly crushingly.

'I did. Anyway, how do you know? You weren't there.'

'You don't have to be there,' said Jake, 'to know when you're romancing. To put it politely. (Some people would call it lying.) The trouble with you is that you don't seem to know the difference between reality and imagination. Which is surprising in one so old as twelve.'

'I do know,' stormed Huck. 'Only I'm a poet so I don't have always to *tell* the truth. What's that all over the floor?' She dabbed a toe in a pool on the linoleum and then crouched down to smell it.

'Your sister threw coffee over me,' said Jake agreeably.

'Why?'

'Because we had a difference of opinion about a matter that it is too tedious to recall now.'

'I'm hungry,' said Huck. 'I wish Mother didn't have to go away. Everyone's so horrid to me when she's not there. What did she leave in the oven for tea?'

'It *was* to have been baked beans, I think. It's hard to tell from the charred remains. She must have gone off early and left the gas too high.'

Huck gave a howl of dismay. 'But I'm *hungry*!'

'So are we all,' said Jake. 'The question is, who's going to do anything about it? Let us consider the matter. There is Edward, who in other and happier times, might have appointed himself the father of this fatherless family, but whose interest in modern life does not go beyond the Middle Ages (except in the cricket season). No, I don't think he will be our cook. There is Polly, the champion of lost causes – will she provide for us in our temporary motherlessness? I am afraid we are not yet a lost enough cause, and in any case charity does not begin at home with Polly. There is Jake – what, Jake? The despair of his schoolmasters, idle, loafing Jake? How could anybody expect anything of him? That leaves us with our twinnies, as different from each other as a platypus from a rhinoceros but twinnies nevertheless. If we left matters to Huck no doubt she would provide an excellent imaginary meal, but not a mouthful to get our teeth into. Which leaves us with Barty, our practical little fellow – if he can mend fuses then surely he can learn to cook.'

Huck ignored all this. 'Where's Mrs B?' she demanded. 'Why isn't she coming in to get our teas like usual? Things always burn if Mother tries to cook them.'

'She and Mother had a difference of opinion,' Jake told her. 'It was unwise of Mother on the eve of her departure, but there it is. Polly would have done exactly the same. It was over a matter of principle, of course, not over a matter of housekeeping.'

'What matter of principle?' said Huck crossly. 'She might have waited till she came back.'

'I think Mother told Mrs B that Mr B ought to be more domestic and help her in the home instead of lording it in the pub, and Mrs B said that she wasn't going to have any interference and she upped and went. I can't say that her teas are much loss.'

'Well, they were something to eat. And nobody else does any cooking.'

It was Barty who went in the end to see what could be done about food. The situation in the kitchen was not promising. Every surface was covered with dirty plates and saucepans and you had to take care as you moved round the floor not to walk into the milk-encrusted saucers that had been put down for the cat and never removed. He peered into cartons that were empty and tins whose contents had been eaten. There seemed to be nothing, and the shop round the corner would be closed now. Huck came in and lolled against the dresser. 'I'm hungry,' she repeated.

'So am I.' Barty dragged up a chair and reached to a cupboard. 'There's butter beans in this packet. What are they?'

Huck bit on one. 'Stones,' she said, spitting it out in disgust.

'Go and ask Polly.'

'She won't know. Anyway, she's arguing with Edward. About politics. American politics. Flinging her arms about.'

'It says on the packet to soak the beans overnight.' Barty slithered down from the chair. 'Do you think if I held them under the tap for a bit it would help?'

'It might.' Huck was bored. 'But do something quickly or I'll die of hunger.' She was leafing through the book that Barty had left lying on the dresser. 'Don't you ever try to make machines? What's the point of drawing them if you never make them? You've got billions of drawings here.'

She returned to the attack later on. They were all sitting round the kitchen table, struggling with the iron-hard beans and some macaroni that Barty, despairing that they would ever soften, had boiled up in the bean water. Hunger had made them all irritable, and though it was accepted that Barty could hardly be blamed, there was a general desire to kick somebody.

'Have you seen Barty's drawings? He just goes on and on planning machines. He never makes them. Isn't it mad?'

'Just about as sane as you telling stories about things that never happened,' remarked Jake. 'Isn't there even any butter we can have with these worms, if there isn't any sauce?' He looked with disgust at the pallid macaroni on his plate.

'They're too short for worms, they're maggots,' said Huck.

'Keep it to yourself then,' said Polly. 'We haven't all got as strong stomachs as you.'

'I don't see why maggots are worse than worms. And it's silly what Jake says. Stories aren't supposed to happen; machines are.'

'Who made that rule?' enquired Jake.

'Everybody knows it.'

Edward spoke up. It was unexpected; he usually stayed outside the Huxtable cut and thrust. 'Why can't Huck make a story that happens and Barty a machine that works?'

'There's a holiday task for you, children,' Jake told them, 'set for you by kind Uncle Edward. (Ed, I thought your nose was turning blue, but I have come to the conclusion that you have been pulling at it with such passion that you have left most of the ink from the newspaper on it. A passing thought.) Now, Bartholomew, now, Hannah, shall we say thank you to Uncle Edward for thinking up this scheme to amuse the little ones?'

This time Huck threw her cup at Jake.

# 2

THE blankets and the pillow in which Barty was burying his head did not shut out the sound of Jake's record player. Nor did they muffle the smell of burning toast which swept under the door.

'Polly says that if you two want any toast you'd better come now,' said Huck, putting her head in officiously.

'I don't want any,' Barty mumbled.

'You'd better come, she's going out, she says, and she wants to tell you about the shopping.'

The kitchen was still thick with the fumes of burnt bread when Barty got down there. Somebody had crumbled bits of it and put it, soaked with milk, on the cat's saucer.

'Thomas *hates* that,' he said, outraged. Thomas was standing there, staring at it, every black hair of him stiff with indignation. Barty took the saucer to the back door and tossed the sodden bits outside.

'You'll have to remember to get some tins of food for him,' said Polly. She was standing by the sink gulping down coffee. 'And we want some stuff for lunch and tea.'

'What shall I get?'

'Oh, I don't know, whatever you think. Get it all put down at Grants'.'

The house was suddenly filled with a silence that felt more obtrusive than the noise. Jake's record had come to an end. He drifted in.

'Somebody from over the road shot an airgun through the window. I shall complain to the police. You going out, Poll? Where to?'

'We're demonstrating at the prison. The prisoners are going on hunger strike and we're supporting them. We're going to mount a picket.'

'To stop them getting out? Or food getting in? A lot of thanks you'll get.'

'Thanks is not what we expect,' said Polly loftily.

Huck looked up from her book. 'I'm going down to the library. I'll take all the tickets anybody has got. Sometimes if that red-haired man's there he lets me take extra books. I'm going to write a poem these holidays too. And not one of those silly ones without rhymes that they let you do at school.'

'And what will it be about, pray?' asked Jake.

'I won't know till I've started. You stop laughing at me – or I'll kill you. You laugh at everything I say.' She charged at him with head lowered.

'Stop it, Huck,' commanded Polly. 'If you break your glasses you might not be able to get them mended before Easter. You going to be around, Jake? Barty wants to know how many he's got to feed at lunch. Edward's digging at St Botolph's but I daresay he'll be back.'

'I might and I might not,' said Jake agreeably. 'I shall probably be experiencing life in Wellington Street.'

'Life!' said Polly contemptuously. 'What you call life is discos and coffee bars.'

'Correct. We aren't all so privileged as you. Besides, there isn't room for all of us outside your prison.'

'If anybody jostles this table again,' said Huck crossly, 'I'm going to . . .'

'Bark? Bite? Bash? Batter?' suggested Jake.

Armed with a carrier bag in either hand, Barty escaped to see what Mrs Grant's shop could produce in the way of supplies. It was not far away, in Wellington Street, which ran past the bottom of the road of

23

terraced nineteenth-century houses where the Huxtables and their much-enduring neighbours lived. It was a seedy little establishment. The windows were opaque with dirt, and you peered through labels advertising Typhoo Tea, Persil and Fairy Soap at faded dummy cartons of custard powder and shredded suet, and rusted tins of soup. The shop had its uses if you did not want to go farther into the city for the ingredients of your next meal. Mrs Grant was also willing to wait to be paid until such time as Mrs Huxtable chose to come to the shop to settle the account. Only Mrs Huxtable could have charmed Mrs Grant into this; she had, as the policeman said, a way with her.

Mrs Grant did not seem to take much part in the business. She sat there, a huge mound of flesh, with her feet up on a stool, and talked to some of the more privileged customers while her son Reg did the running about – a small, sulky, plump man with thin red curls that seemed to be slipping off the back of his head.

'Well,' said Reg impatiently, 'what's your mum wanting today? She's quicker than you at choosing, I'll say that for her.'

'She's not here,' said Barty. 'I want something for our lunch. I was thinking.'

'Better have baked beans and be done with it. That's what she always gives 'em.'

'I thought we'd have a change and try something new.' Barty stared round at all the tins, hoping for inspiration. 'What's that like?' He pointed to a label which showed green peppers stuffed with rice.

Reg glanced briefly. 'Never touch the muck. We got it in for the university students. But they don't seem to fancy it. It wouldn't be in your mum's line.'

'I wanted something *different*,' said Barty hopelessly. 'Something sort of tasty and nice. Not baked beans.'

'Fish fingers then. Or that tinned ravioli stuff – though I wouldn't touch it with a barge pole myself. Filthy foreign mess.'

'What do *you* have?' Barty asked boldly. 'For your dinner, I mean.'

'Dad cooks ours,' said Reg contemptuously. 'Proper food, he gives us. Not tins or the deep freeze.'

Mrs Grant put a word in. 'Daddy's at it now, I daresay. In fact I was thinking I could smell the onions he was frying for the steak. Of course I could do it just as well,' she added, giving Barty a sharp look. 'But I have to think of my career. A girl owes it to herself, that's what I always say. And Daddy understands.' She heaved one leg over another and smoothed the pink nylon overall over her vast expanse of front. 'I could just fancy something now to be going on with,' she said dreamily. 'Something *nice*. Reg, reach us down a packet of gipsy creams.'

'Mr Grant does the cooking?' Barty was amazed. He had not even realized there was a Mr Grant.

'Always has done, always will, I daresay,' said Reg shortly. 'He likes it. Mum and I don't. Now, have you made up your mind?'

Barty left the shop with a full carrier bag. By the turning to Simon Street a black scurrying figure paused, hesitated, walked on, then thought better of it and came back. This was Father Fabian, the rector of St Wulfstan, who, though the Huxtables played a dominant part in his congregation, had never conquered his nervousness of them.

'Been doing the shopping, I see?'

'Yes,' said Barty. Then, as there was a long silence which Father Fabian did not seem able to fill, he thought he had better add to this monosyllable. 'Mother is in America.'

Father Fabian's face took on a hunted look as of one

who felt that something was now expected of him. 'You managing all right?'

'I think so. She'll be back for Easter. The police have got our money.'

'That's right, that's right,' said Father Fabian heartily. 'The police have always been good friends of yours. Well, I'd better be on my way now. Remember you can always call in at the Rectory if you need anything,' he called back over his shoulder, with the great relief of one who felt that the correct courtesies had been exchanged.

Barty, too, was relieved. Father Fabian's nervousness was infectious, but there were moments when conversation with him could not be avoided. He put his bags down and stretched his cramped hands. Through the forest of guitars in the huge plate glass windows of Music Magic opposite he could make out the figures of Jake and one of his friends, leaning against the counter, talking to the boy behind it. When the manager of the shop got tired of his junior assistant wasting his time in this way, he would throw out Jake who would then move on to stare at the shirts and ties in the Wizard of Oz, or finger the objects in The Gloryhole where you could buy anything from joss sticks to clockwork mice or posters. And then there was always the coffee bar next door. Wellington Street could provide Jake with amusement for most of the holidays.

Once round the corner in Simon Street Barty loitered, staring in at the windows that obligingly did not have net curtains. He liked best to look in the early evening when the lights were just on. Then he could see in to the front rooms, lovely tidy ones with pretty furniture and wallpaper. Sometimes, if he was lucky, he might even catch a glimpse of a family sitting at a meal and eating as if they were enjoying their food.

The Huxtable front door stood out, not because of its

colour but because of its lack of it. Nobody had bothered to do anything about it since Huck had once lit a pool of paraffin on the pavement to see what would happen. She had spent a month in hospital after that, and the experiment had also burnt out a car which unfortunately had belonged to the City Education Officer. He was new to the area and had asked tiresome questions about Huck not being at school – a matter which those who knew the reputation of the Huxtables would not have taken up.

Barty always winced when he looked at that charred wood – it would be so lovely to have a glossy front door with a brass knocker. He carried his bags into the kitchen. The house was quite still. Huck would be at the library; Polly was picketing, Jake was in Wellington Street, and Edward was helping to excavate the foundations of old houses near St Botolph's. There was only Thomas to greet him, mewing hungrily and walking on tiptoe round and round his legs.

He opened a tin of cat food, then began the tidying up. This was difficult because the rooms were crammed with Huxtable possessions. Their mother, Mary Huxtable, had married her first cousin, James (it was said because she could not endure the thought of changing her name), and the family had always clung to its past. Old school photographs of their father, pictures of their grandfathers and grandmothers, great uncles and great aunts crowded the walls, with Huck's and Jake's earliest splashy paintings pinned below them. There were gaudy tasselled football caps that somebody had won at school seventy or eighty years before, miniatures of small Huxtables of the past, pictures of houses they had lived in, posters of Mrs Huxtable's political meetings. And every hobby that had held the fancy of present day Huxtables had left its mark, from the holes in the door where they

27

had played darts one Christmas, to the oil on the wall which marked where Polly had once leaned her bike when she was trying to repair a puncture.

Barty made fitful attempts to bring some order into the rooms, gave it up, and then sat down to look at his latest catalogue of electronic supplies and to plan how he would lay out £50 should they ever come his way. It was totally absorbing. He did not raise his head until the front door burst open, and then, sitting tensely, he heard a torrent of feet pour down the hall. Polly came in.

'Oh, you're here. I thought there'd be some food around. What can we have that's quick? We've got to go back and picket in minus five minutes.'

'There's stuff in a carrier bag,' muttered Barty.

'Come and show us then.'

The kitchen was full of girls who seemed to be copies of Polly – tall, energetic, with flopping fair hair. Barty fumbled in the bag. 'I got some spaghetti in a tin, but I haven't put it to get hot yet.'

'We can't wait for it then, we're due back.'

'Little Polly Flinders made policemen into cinders,' sang Jake from behind. 'Polly put the kettle on, Polly put the pickets on – they've all gone away.'

'You shut up or you'll get clobbered,' said Polly mildly.

'There's cornflakes,' said one of the picketing party. 'Let's have that. With cocoa and sugar on top. Here's some cocoa. Oh, no, it isn't either.' She held up a dirty pink suspender, 'unless it's the sort of cocoa that Huxtables drink.'

There were hyena laughs as girls crowded round and examined the object. Nobody heard Barty's explanation. 'I found it on the floor, I think it must have been Mrs B's.'

'Now, now,' said Jake from behind. 'Handle it carefully. It's a vital and delicate part of Barty's latest electronic device.'

The whole pack of them seemed to turn on him. 'What's the gadget this time, Barty? A remote control device for doing homework? Something to detect saturation point in the way of dirty dishes? A door-answering machine to deal with the neighbours' complaints? Is that bit of old pram outside your front door anything to do with it?'

Through the jabber and the screeches of laughter Huck's voice rang like a bell. 'He's brought a machine home this time. From the rubbish tip. It's a Time Machine – for going into the past and the future – and he's put it in Mother's bedroom.'

# 3

BARTY stared out of the window. He was in Huck's room, at the top of the house, as far away as he could get from the yammering, screeching mob in the kitchen. Below him was a chequered pattern of walls that divided up the tiny squares that the Simon Street householders called their gardens, and that were no use to anyone except possibly the cats. He could see Thomas on the wall now, his tail curled round him, musing and dozing, well away from Huxtable hubbub. He wished he could escape from it too; he wished he belonged to any family in the world but the Huxtables.

Someone threw open the door. 'What are you doing here?' said Huck, in the tone of voice of someone who doesn't particularly want to know. 'I want library tickets.' She was poking and clattering and pulling open drawers. 'You're *crying*!' She stared at him inquisitively. 'Are you feeling ill? Anyway, it can't be appendicitis, you've had it out.'

Barty kept his face turned away and stared out of the window. The walls below shimmered and winked through the tears that he tried to keep from falling.

'Are you missing Mother?' said Huck incredulously. 'She often goes away. And she'll be back soon.'

'Those people!' said Barty furiously. The discovery that he could hardly speak clearly made him angrier still. 'Standing around and yapping and laughing. And why'd you got to go and start them all off again talking about time machines? I thought they'd never leave me alone. It's bad enough having to listen to you reading all that stuff.' The tears of rage at the way he had been humiliated nearly choked him.

'I like that!' shrieked Huck. 'Me wearing myself out trying to amuse you and getting you to read proper books instead of advertisements and catalogues when I could be writing poetry! Anyway, it is a Time Machine. You didn't know what it was, well, I'm telling you now. It's a Time Machine, like the one Wells writes about in the book. It just came to me in a flash – I suddenly knew.'

'I don't know what you're talking about. Get your old library tickets and get out!' He turned on her savagely.

'I'm not going to get out, it's my room, isn't it? And I'm going to take you downstairs and *prove* that it's a Time Machine. Oh, come on, the others have gone now. I'll get the book.'

Mrs Huxtable's room looked as though it had been left in a great hurry. Dusk last night had masked the chaos. Now Barty shivered in the chill of a room that felt as if it had been long unoccupied, and stared at the clothes tumbled over the bed, the drawers that gaped open, the litter of papers on the dressing table. In the middle of it all, where he had left it by the bed, stood the dirt-encrusted maze of rods. Remorse swept over him, mixed with a sudden longing for his mother's warm, cheerful presence. How could he have brought this bit of rubbish into her room? He took a step towards the object, meaning to scoop it up and carry it downstairs, but Huck, coming in at that moment, gave a shout of protest.

'You leave it there, otherwise you'll have Jake poking around with it. Now listen to what the book says.' She squatted down on the rug with the battered, greasy copy of H. G. Wells that had been time-stained even when their father had picked it up for a shilling twenty years

31

ago. ' "A glittering metallic framework" . . . "parts were of nickel, parts of ivory, parts had certainly been filed or sawn out of rock-crystal" – Barty, you're not listening!'

Barty was on the point of disappearing through the door. 'It's her passport,' he shouted from the stairs. 'I've just remembered.' He was back in a moment, his face distraught. 'It's not there.'

'She must have taken it, of course,' said Huck with irritation. 'Don't you need it for America?'

'She wouldn't know where it was. She gave it to me last time she came back from being abroad because there'd been all that fuss at the airport about her forgetting it, and she said to put it in a safe place and to be sure to see that she had it next time she went. So I put it behind the clock in the bookroom. But I didn't know she was going to America yesterday and she didn't know it was there and anyway it's disappeared. What are we going to do? Do they put people in prison for not having passports? Or perhaps they won't let her back into England again!'

Huck was impatient. 'It must be all right otherwise she would have telephoned or something. She probably looked behind the clock.'

'She didn't know where I put it, I tell you.'

'Oh, do stop fussing.' Huck dismissed the subject. 'Come and look at this machine. What did you want to bring it home for if you can't be interested?'

'You keep reading that stuff from the book. It doesn't tell you anything.'

'Of course it does. It says how there are four dimensions, Length, Breadth, Thickness and Time, and how if you could get the geometry right you could move in time like you do in space. It's scientific – I thought you liked science.'

'Scientific!' said Barty contemptuously.

32

'The Time Traveller's friends were like you, then he got on his machine and disappeared.'

'Of course he could, in a book.'

'You think that nothing is real unless you can touch it and see it,' said Huck scornfully. 'What about radio and television then? You can't see sound waves and light waves or whatever they are, coming through the air, can you? Well then, you can't see Time either, but it doesn't mean that you couldn't invent something to move through it. Once people thought it was impossible to fly. They talked about the moon as if going there was a silly dream. And now look.' There was no reasoning with Huck in this mood; she was mesmerized by her own oratory, convinced by her own arguments. 'And this is a Time Machine. Don't ask me how I know. I just do.'

'Go on then, make it work,' said Barty wearily.

'It won't yet. There's something missing, I don't know what but there is.' She considered it, frowning. 'I know. The book says there should be ivory starting levers, and a quartz rod. I can see where they go but they aren't there. Come and look.'

Barty slouched over. Huck was pointing to two sockets, one on the rod that supported the saddle frame, and the other opposite, below what looked like handlebars. 'They've got earth in them now, but I bet you that's where the quartz rod went, like the crossbar on a man's bike. What is quartz? He calls it rock-crystal too, it's got to be something twinkly. And there's the ivory time handles. They go there and there – don't you see? Find me a nail file or some scissors, I'm going to get the dirt out. Where is there ivory in this house?'

'I've got some,' Barty found himself saying, to his surprise. As often happened, he had been sucked into the game by the force of Huck's personality. 'Do you remember that baby elephant's tusk carved like a crocodile that Mother brought back last time she was in Africa?'

When he came back Huck had cleared the clogged earth from the hollow ends of the rods that seemed to be intended for the operator of the Machine to grip as handles; they were grooved, presumably to stop hands from slipping. She blew away the last of the grit and pushed in the tail of the crocodile. 'You see how it fits,' she said triumphantly. 'The trouble is, there should be two, one for the past, one for the future. But you can push this one backwards and forwards, so perhaps we can manage with one. Now, there's just this crystal bar. And I'm sure that's the most important thing, the real part that makes it work. It must be still in the rubbish dump. Can you remember where you found the rest of it?'

The east wind made their eyes water as they emerged on the Meadow some twenty minutes later and bit through Barty's anorak as they plodded along the raised concrete track that took the dustcarts to the tip. At this end the spring floods had not yet subsided; there was a white sheet of water with tussocks thrusting up through it, on the edge of which a few shaggy ponies tugged at the coarse scanty grass, their tails blown round them by the wind.

'You're walking on history here,' remarked Huck conversationally, 'all these layers of rubbish. Don't you feel it?'

'I'm too cold.'

'You're too thick, that's what you mean. It must be awful to be as unimaginative as you.'

'I don't want to be like you. No wonder your school reports say you're potty.'

'They don't say so. They say,' Huck preened herself, 'that I have a highly original mind.'

'It means the same thing. Only they don't like to say so to Mother.'

'It means I've got genius,' said Huck complacently.

Barty looked at her helplessly as she marched along with her tousled curls beaten back by the wind. You could never argue with Huck, you just had to accept that she thought along completely different lines from anybody else, and never at any point could your line and hers touch. Today she was wearing somebody's old black velvet dress, bought at a church jumble sale. It was far too long, and she had to hold it up with both hands, as well as try to keep a shawl round her shoulders.

'That dress smells,' he said crossly. 'They always do from St Wulfstan.'

'It's mothball, I like it. One day I want to buy a pound of mothballs and eat them like imperial mints.'

'How are you going to get over the gate in it?'

They had reached the five-bar gate with the barbed wire on top and the notice that said 'unauthorized entry forbidden'. The concrete track here bridged a murky, stagnant ditch which was fringed as far as the eye could see with a line of willows. As Barty looked at them waves of desolation broke over him. Last year Mother had come with them to pick willow catkins to decorate the church for Easter, and now there was an ocean between them and her exuberant presence.

Huck, however, was thinking only of the gate. 'I can hitch it up to get over. You put your anorak over the barbed wire for me. Now, where's this hole you said you dug yesterday?'

But that was the trouble. Barty had thought he knew exactly how far he had walked from the gate and could easily spot the hollow that he had scooped out. But the ground was pitted with holes on either side of the track. He seemed to recognize one, only to spot another a few yards away which might equally well have been his.

He shook his head dolefully. 'I don't know. It all looks the same now.'

'We'll have to try divining then,' said Huck briskly. 'We can't dig everywhere, it would take centuries. Go and get a forked twig from those trees. Oh, I suppose I'd better come with you, otherwise you won't know what sort.'

The trees were on the edge of the ditch by the gate, and it was as uninviting as ever a ditch could be, clotted with rusty tins and plastic bottles, clouded here and there with a film of oil. But Barty found himself trying to scramble along the muddy bank, holding with icy hands to the wire fence while Huck shouted directions.

'Not that tree. No, go on a bit farther, that's not the right one. The next one, the branch just above your head.'

Barty stretched up with one hand and tore at a twig. Then he gave a screech. 'My foot's gone in!'

Huck glanced in his direction. 'It's only one foot.'

'But it's up to my knee. And it's icy cold. And it *stinks*.'

'You've got a good twig anyway,' said Huck with satisfaction. 'I can do things with this.' She tested the twig, bending it this way and that, while Barty tried to wipe some of the mud off his shoe and his jeans with a bunch of grass.

'Water diviners use hazel,' he said crossly. 'That's hornbeam. The *smell*! It's all through my jeans.'

'I don't want to divine water, do I? Hornbeam's special, I think it's a witch sort of tree. I knew I was choosing something special when I told you to get it. Oh, come along before all the goodness goes, I can feel it oozing away.'

Still lamenting, with his sodden shoe making squelching noises as he limped, Barty followed Huck as she marched down the track, balancing the twig delicately between finger and thumb, with a fixed expression of concentration. Presently she plunged off the path into the hummocks by the side. In time grass would grow there, but now the ground was bare. It might have been a battlefield over which survivors had struggled to toss a little earth, leaving rusted iron and discarded boots pointing up at the sky, and here and there a glove, like a dead man's hand, dumbly gesticulating.

'It wasn't anywhere like as far over as this,' Barty shouted into the wind.

'Shut up, can't you!' Her voice came thinly back. She was zigzagging, sometimes tripping and stumbling, sometimes plunging up to her knees in drifts of dead leaves, but always, it seemed, with a sense of purpose. From a few yards behind, where he had stopped for a moment to try to scrape off some of the leaves that stuck to his wet shoe, Barty saw her throw up her arm and yell. When he caught up she was grubbing away like a mole.

'It's gone, my divining twig. Don't stand there; help me.'

Round them was bare earth. There were cinders and bits of broken glass and china, but of the hornbeam, which had been quite a large twig, there was no sign.

Barty peered all round. 'It can't have gone far. What are you digging for? It can't have buried itself.'

'Sometimes I think you're worse than Lucy Soper,' said Huck passionately. 'I'm not bothering about the twig now. I've found the place, I tell you, and I'm getting something, I feel it.' With an expression of intense concentration, Huck was fumbling deep in the earth. 'It's stuck down there and I can't get hold of enough to pull. Help me – what does it matter about your hands getting dirty?'

It took a lot of effort to free whatever it was. Below

the loose top surface the earth was more tightly packed and the object was deeply embedded in it. Barty's fingers felt frozen, and grit was driven deep down his nails, but he scratched away with a sharp-ended bit of slate. The hole grew deeper, but still Huck's furious efforts to prise out what she wanted were unsuccessful.

Barty peered in. 'We don't know how big it is. There may be yards more still buried.'

'Then you'll have to dig deeper. Go home and get a spade or shovel or something.' Huck had both hands wrapped round it and was pulling and straining. Suddenly she was sprawled flat on her back, but clasping triumphantly a long glassy object which, in spite of the dirt and earth that encrusted it, twinkled and flashed so that it almost seemed to be moving in her hands. 'The rock-crystal,' she said, looking at it gloatingly. 'I didn't know what that was before, but I know now. Come on, hurry, I want to get home and try it.'

Huck, when she wanted to, could walk so fast that it was difficult to keep up. Barty tried to peer over her shoulder at the object as she strode down Meadow Street with her skirts hitched up for greater speed under the shawl now knotted round her waist. It seemed to be a carved glass rod, so cut that even on this grey day the light struck at its surfaces and glanced off them as if it were a diamond.

'Good,' said Huck as she stood in the hall again. 'There's nobody in. You need peace for this. Go and find something we can scrape dirt off with.'

When Barty came upstairs with a kitchen knife and newspapers to cover the floor Huck was polishing the bar with a headscarf. 'I've just washed it. It doesn't so much matter about the rest of the thing being dirty but this must be bright.'

'That's Mother's *hat*,' said Barty, outraged. 'What she

wears to weddings and funerals.'

'You could always wash it. But she wouldn't mind, you know how she hates going to weddings. Stop nagging, and help me fit this bar in.'

The extraordinary thing was that it did fit, miraculously. It almost jumped into place. Before either of them was conscious of pushing it into the two holes, it was there, solid and immovable. Until then, the object had certainly been impressively complex, precision made, but it had still looked like something that had spent a long time on a rubbish tip. Now it was transformed into what might even have been called a working piece of machinery – if only it had any parts that could actually move and if only they knew how to use it. There was something unnerving about the way the crystal bar flashed, as though a live current was being passed through it. Barty instinctively took a step back.

'Now,' said Huck with satisfaction, 'the only problem is this dial. I suppose it's to measure the time, but the trouble is the figures have worn off. I think it had better be days at first while we're still experimenting. I'm sure I saw a bit of stamp paper somewhere. Look, there it is; write "days" on it and stick it on. And I can't sit on the saddle without something to cover it, those springs would cut me in half.' She seized a cushion to cover the framework of springs. 'Don't look at me all soupily like that. I made the cushion myself about three Christmases ago, so I'm sure Mother wouldn't mind.'

She straddled the crystal bar and sat down gingerly on the cushion. 'Of course we don't know whether this ivory handle is for the past or for the future. But if I pull it towards me that means the past, don't you think?'

'How on earth can I know?'

'I thought at least you'd know that much. What's the use of you fooling round with machines all the time if you can't tell me that. I'll move the dial hand back, just a snick. Now, wish me luck. You ought to be breaking a bottle of champagne or something.'

'Take care!' said Barty, he didn't know why.

But Huck was not there, nor was the Machine. Giddily he reeled back on to the bed. He distinctly remembered, later, staring at the earth on the floor where the Machine had stood. Stupefied, he stooped down to see whether by any possibility Huck and the Machine were under the bed, and bumped his head painfully on a sharp point.

'Look out,' said Huck. 'What are you doing? That's the time lever. You'll be knocking me back into the past again and I want my tea.'

# 4

'JUMBO wants to see us,' announced Polly, returning to the kitchen from the telephone, 'all of us.'

The five of them were there, eating their breakfast together for a wonder, propped against the dresser or sitting at the table, according to their dispositions.

'As friend or police superintendent?' Jake had his chair tipped back and was dipping a finger in the jam. 'I mean, are any of us in trouble that we know of? I'm not, for one, but I don't know what you others have been up to. Yesterday's evening paper said something about Polly and her gang biting a policeman.'

Polly dismissed Jake's remarks as unworthy of discussion. 'He said he wanted to see us and count us before he turned us loose for the holidays. He also said that somebody had been phoning the police station yesterday when he was out and leaving messages about Mother's passport, and what was it all about?'

'That was me,' said Barty. 'She hasn't got it, but I don't know where it is and I wanted to know what we ought to do.'

Huck lifted her head for a moment from the exercise book where she was scribbling. 'She's got it now.'

Barty stared at her. 'What do you mean? How could she?'

'Well, she has. So stop interrupting, I'm trying to write.'

Barty stared at her, frustrated and puzzled. She had been like this since yesterday afternoon, snappy and secretive, and – which was most unlike Huck – unwilling to talk.

'You'd better sort it out before we get there,' said Polly. 'Jumbo doesn't like having his time wasted. And we'll have to get some of the money from him while we're about it, we need some more food. I suppose we can all go, by the way? What's everybody doing this morning?'

'I doubt whether plans have been laid yet,' said Jake, licking round his finger to get off the last of the jam. 'Except possibly by Huck who is deeply involved in an ode to Time.'

'It's not *to* Time, it's about it. And don't laugh either, I'll probably get the Nobel Prize one day.'

'The Peace Prize?' said Jake. 'I hardly think so, Huck, my love. They don't seem to care for little girls who knock down other little girls with their heads.'

'The Poetry Prize, of course. Can you think of a good rhyme for dazzle?'

'Razzle,' suggested Jake. ' "Mine eyes dazzle, I have been on the razzle." '

'It doesn't scan,' said Huck with scorn.

Polly paid no attention to all this. 'What are we going to eat today? Grants' don't have things like sausages or chops – I'm getting sick of all their food. Heaven knows what they eat themselves.'

'Mr Grant does all the cooking for Mrs Grant,' said Barty. 'She likes to have her career, she says.'

Jake gave a screech of laughter. 'I hope you heard that one, Poll. You and Mrs Grant are twin souls, it seems.'

'Can't you ever be serious, just for one minute?' said Polly impatiently.

'Not for one second, when you're around.'

'All I can say is it's lucky one of us has a sense of duty. Now look, we'd better go, they're expecting me at the prison any minute. Put that book down, Ed, and come on. Jumbo wants us all, and we've got to collect some money.'

Sighing, Edward stood up. 'Where did you say we'd got to go?'

'To the police station. To collect money – cash, dough, lolly, brass, tin,' said Jake slowly and distinctly. 'I have even heard it called oof, but I somehow doubt whether you would know it by that name.'

'If it's the police station that's all right. I can go on to St Botolph's afterwards. They're digging there, and I've heard there may be some medieval tiles.'

'The notion of our Ed digging is enough to make even Thomas smile through his whiskers. Still I suppose you've got to do something before the Australians arrive and unpack their cricket-bags. But do you know which end up to hold your spade?'

'Oh, chuck it, Jake,' said Polly, 'you're not as clever as you think you are. Come on, Barty, don't fuss with the washing up, there's all the morning to do it in afterwards.'

'Now, how clever do you think I think I am?' Jake enquired. 'It is an interesting topic and one we could fruitfully pursue.'

The five of them moved down Cornmarket Street towards the police station, Edward striding ahead, his forehead creased, his lips moving as he apparently pondered some cosmic problem; Polly and Jake wrangling in ringing voices as they went, totally oblivious of the irritation of the passers-by whom they elbowed aside as they loudly argued, and then Huck, huddled dourly in her shawl, with Barty running to catch her up.

People in the street nudged each other : 'There go the Huxtables.' It was not often, in fact, that all five of them could be seen together. Everybody in the district knew about them and had an anecdote to tell about them.

There had been a long line of Huxtables there for two hundred years or more; Huxtable monuments could be found in the city churches, portraits of them in various of the colleges; there was one in the Lord Mayor's parlour, and a set of caricatures of Q. E. Huxtable, the original absent-minded professor, in the university museum. Their activities had been wide-ranging. One had been a bishop, another hanged for horse-stealing (though this was exceptional). Some had fought passionately for their fellow men, others had been content to be eccentrics, but most of them had somehow or other made their mark in the town. However, when people said 'the Huxtables' nowadays, they meant the five children who, dressed apparently from Oxfam cast-offs, and engaged in highly individualistic activities, were as much of a tourist attraction as the dignitaries in their academic robes seen solemnly processing to some university function or another.

At last Barty got near enough to Huck to grab her shoulder.

'Huck, you've got to tell me about the passport.'

'I gave it to her. Yesterday.' And Huck, as if she wanted to put an end to the topic, strode on faster than ever.

She could be very tiresome. 'What am I going to say to Jumbo then when he asks about the telephone message?' he shouted over the heads of a surprised pair of girls who were considering the sandals in Peter Lord's windows.

'Say what you like,' said Huck over her shoulder.

He pushed his way through the window-gazers. 'You've got to be serious. Passports are important.'

'Who isn't being serious? And if I told you what had happened you wouldn't believe me. Well then, I gave it to her by Time Machine.'

'By Time Machine?'

'There you are, you don't believe me.' Huck pressed her lips firmly together as though she were determined to say no more, but it was not in her to keep silent. 'You know yesterday when I got on the Time Machine?' she burst out. 'How long did it seem I was away?'

'Away?' Barty stared at her. When she had a story to tell she usually swung into it with enormous verve and drama; she didn't hint at it and stop and start like this.

'It felt like half an hour to me, but it can't have been because you didn't ask any questions about where I'd gone.'

'I'll tell you what was peculiar,' said Barty slowly. 'I did think for a moment that you'd disappeared – you and the Machine. Then I bent down to look under the bed and I nearly knocked you over, so you were there all the time.'

'But I wasn't, you see,' said Huck triumphantly; the story teller had now asserted itself. 'Shall I tell you what happened? I got on the Machine. Right? I moved the dial hand back just a little and I pulled the ivory towards me. Then the Machine started moving. It was a funny feeling because the night went past me. It got gradually dark, and then it was all black, like going through a tunnel; then I could see the shapes of furniture and things, then it was properly light, but noises seemed to be rushing past me. Then they stopped. Everything was just the same, I was in Mother's bedroom, but you weren't there. I didn't know what had happened, I thought I might have fainted – when I fainted that time I fell downstairs it felt as though centuries and centuries had rolled over me. There was someone moving round the house downstairs, so I went to the top of the stairs and shouted. It was Mother.'

'Mother?' repeated Barty.

'Yes, it was the day before yesterday, you see, so she hadn't gone yet. I went downstairs and then I remembered about the passport. It was where you said, behind the clock in the bookroom. She was just going out through the door. She had that black zip bag all bulging with stuff and I pushed it in the top. She said she didn't know anybody would be back from school yet, and to give her love to you all and say that tea was in the oven. Then she was gone and the house felt very lonely and so I came back.'

'Are you two going to walk into the river?' Jake shouted at them. 'We're going to the police station, not out swimming.'

For years the police had taken unofficial charge of the Huxtables, for, whether their mother was home or not, and although she was warmly affectionate, her mind did tend to drift on to other matters. It was the police who took them to hospital to be stitched up after their frequent accidents, picked them out of fights, and brought them home when they were young enough to get lost. They were so much a part of the police station that they were invited to the Christmas parties for the police children – the best tea of the year, Huck said. And even though Edward and Polly were in theory quite old enough to run the family while their mother was away, Jumbo, the superintendent who had appointed himself their chief guardian, insisted on seeing them all from time to time so that he could count them to make sure they were all alive. He also took over the money. (He had done this since the time when Polly, aged twelve, had run off with the lot and had been found at London Airport, trying to make her way to China to join the Communist Party.)

But he was often difficult to catch, and when they got there today he was out. 'He'll be back in five to ten minutes,' said the young policeman in charge of the front office. 'He'll see you then. And don't you go fretting,' he remarked to Polly. 'The prison walls will stand up for a bit without you.'

'Polly doesn't want them to stand up,' said Jake amiably. 'She'd like them to fall flat. But I think we'll wait outside, thank you; the smell of the disinfectant that you use here rather jangles the nerves, and the wall decorations,' (he waved his hand towards the notices about bicycle thieves and housebreakers and Colorado beetle and swine fever) 'tend to depress the lay mind.'

They went and sat on a wall in the nearby war memorial gardens. It was a sheltered place. Huck lay back on the rock plants. She had relapsed into brooding, and lay there staring up at the sky.

'Do you think I fainted?' she said suddenly to Barty. 'You know how you do have those peculiar dreams when you faint? They go on and on and you feel all giddy when you wake up. I felt giddy.'

'You didn't faint,' said Barty cautiously. 'At least, you didn't fall down.'

'Perhaps you can faint without that. Don't people have blackouts or something? But then there's the passport. You say she couldn't have known where it was, and I did find it and gave it to her. And she must have got it because she hasn't telephoned or telegrammed or anything to say bring it to the airport. So it must have been the Time Machine after all.' She was working herself back into her state of excitement.

Barty, as always, attended only to the practical points. 'What are we going to say to Jumbo about the passport? I did telephone him and now he's going to ask all sorts of questions. I hate it when he starts asking questions like a policeman. It makes me feel like a criminal.'

'You just say you made a mistake,' said Huck im-

47

patiently. 'Just don't start getting hot and bothered, that's all, then he won't ask questions.'

Jake now diverted their attention. 'I say, there's an old gent on the path who seems to be exceedingly excited. Do you think by any chance he's addressing us?'

Only Huxtables, absorbed in their own talk, could have failed to notice him before; he looked very angry indeed. He had a red face, bristling white whiskers, glassy eyes and no neck to speak of. Beside him was a sad gaunt lady who stood there, expressionless, staring into space, as if these explosions of wrath were so much a part of her life that she had ceased to notice them.

'Can't you answer when you're spoken to?' shouted the man from the footpath.

'Yes, if we hear,' said Jake with sweet reason.

'You hear now. Don't you see there's a notice forbidding the public to walk on the grass?'

Huck sat up. 'Yes, I can see it. It's over there.'

'And you mean to sit there defying it?' He was getting dangerously angry now. His face looked like a balloon that was soon going to burst. But the Huxtables just stared at him with interest. They had never allowed angry bellowing men to shake them from what they wanted to do. Especially men who argued as badly as this one did.

'If we sit here we are hardly walking,' said Edward courteously.

'Nor can you prove we're defying anything,' added Polly.

'And didn't you see that notice saying that the keepers had orders to turn out people wearing ragged or unseemly clothing? And just look at you!'

This made Polly very angry in her turn. She was on the point of delivering one of her political lectures, but Jake got in first.

'*I* was always taught when I was a little boy that personal remarks were rude. I don't know what the old people are coming to these days, I'm sure,' he said, smiling engagingly.

'And as for you,' shouted the man, angrily brandishing his stick, 'you young jackanapes, you ought to be arrested. Going around with hair like that, you're an offence to public decency, that's what you are.'

'As a matter of fact,' remarked Jake, standing up, 'we are on our way to the police station now. So we will pass on your remarks to the superintendent.'

They ambled behind the couple on their way out from the gardens. The man was loudly addressing his silent companion. The Huxtables could hear every word. 'It's all the fault of modern education. Makes them too soft — panders to them – no discipline. That's what they want, discipline, the birch, toeing the line, respect for their elders. The old public schools knew what they were about, by George!'

The Huxtables caught him up at the iron gates that led on to the street. Jake bowed. 'We have duly digested your remarks and we will keep them by us for reference. Goodbye – so very glad to have made your acquaintance.'

The superintendent was in his office now, it seemed. 'Is it Uncle Jumbo today?' Jake casually asked the constable on duty, 'or Jumbo, yes sir, no sir, if you please, I have been a very wicked boy, sir?'

'You get along there quick and don't keep him waiting. None of your lip, neither.'

But Jumbo looked pleased to see them. It seemed that the family was not in for one of the lectures that he periodically administered. He sat there massively in his chair, smiling benevolently, a vast man with a craggy face and a broken nose – not a professional battle scar but a relic of a cricket match many years before. His subordinates may have had some reason in complaining that he was hardly like a copper – he had decorated the walls of his room (painted in the usual institutional dirty cream) with tiny reproductions in gilt frames of Van Gogh's sunflowers and Degas's ballet dancers.

'Well, and how are you all shaping? Everything in good order? What have you been doing with yourselves?'

'I've been cheeking senior citizens,' said Jake agreeably, 'and observing life in Wellington Street. Edward's digging up the past, Polly's been waving banners outside the prison and biting your policemen – but I expect you know that.'

Huck interrupted. 'Does Polly bite people? I thought she only talked. I wouldn't mind politics if I could bite people.'

'Wait till the summer,' Jake told her. 'You'll only get a mouthful of wool if you try now. It's more satisfying when the weather is warmer and people are wearing fewer clothes.'

'You'd better keep off my men,' said the superintendent. 'There's a limit to even their patience. And what do the little ones do?'

'If you mean us,' said Huck, 'we're not little. I'm writing a poem.'

'Poems is it? It was a story last time. The longest story there ever was, longer than those TV serials you said, and they seem to be a lifetime and more. That one of Henry VIII, for instance – you'd have said there'd been sixty wives, not six. Though it had its moments, I suppose.'

'There was a man outside with a wife,' said Huck suddenly.

'Was there, now?'

Huck fingered the pencils that lay in the tray on Jumbo's desk and looked dreamily into space. 'I'm sure he beat her, she looked so sad and thin – like his prisoner, really. Anyway, she stood there beside him and he was in a terrible passion, waving his stick and shouting.'

'At her?'

'No, at us,' said Huck with satisfaction. 'Because we were on the grass, or something. And Jake answered him back and then he got really mad and he lifted his stick and was going to attack Jake. Then it was really exciting, she caught his arm, "Don't, Henry, I implore you," she said, "beat me if you like, but spare this innocent child, for the sake of our own dead son!" And then he turned on her and I thought he was going to kill her, so I ran . . .'

'Is this really true?' the superintendent asked the others.

'Bits are,' said Jake. 'But it's not one of her best. Not vintage Huck, I would say.'

'No, I thought "spare the innocent child" was putting it a bit strong – particularly if the innocent child was supposed to be you.'

'You oughtn't to interrupt,' raged Huck, 'it's like waking up something that's been hibernating. I'm sure you could kill people that way.'

Nobody took any notice, they were used to Huck. 'And what has Barty been doing?' enquired the superintendent. 'He seems the odd one out somehow.'

Huck spoke for him. 'He is. He doesn't really like us.'

'Sometimes I'm not surprised,' said Jumbo.

'People ought to be fond of their families,' pursued Huck primly. 'He just wants to be neat and tidy; he'd like to tidy us away into drawers if he could, and then settle down to draw machines. He'd rather be an only child,' she added with ineffable scorn.

'So would I, if I had to live in the same house as you. Now what about this message about a passport?'

It was the moment that Barty had been dreading. Already mortified by Huck's attack, he floundered miserably. 'I thought she hadn't got it. I put it in a place where she didn't know it was.' Any moment now, he thought, Jumbo would turn into the superintendent questioning a prisoner.

'It's quite all right,' said Huck smoothly. 'She's got it. I know because I gave it to her.'

Jumbo looked at Barty, by now crimson with confusion. 'I daresay it is all right, you know; you'd surely have heard by now otherwise. Well, to change the subject, are you needing any money? Your mother's left a fair bit this time – to cover emergencies, I suppose. Who does the cooking?'

'It's no good looking at Polly,' Jake pointed out. 'She could tell you what prisoners eat, but not what we're going to have. And Edward moves on a higher plane altogether, I doubt whether he ever notices what he's eating. As for me . . .'

The superintendent cut through all this. 'As for you, you'd talk the hind legs off a donkey and then start on the front ones, and the same goes for Huck. That leaves Barty. Can you take over the housekeeping then, Barty?'

'He does very well at it,' said Edward. 'He gave us – what was it we had for supper last night?' He looked appealingly at the rest of the family.

'Fish fingers,' said Huck sulkily. 'I don't call that doing well.'

'But none of you feels inclined to try to do better. What a lot you are!' The superintendent leaned back in his chair and sighed. 'Still, you stick together, I'll say that, and you're all still alive.'

'I wonder if we'd have done better if we'd have been a hundred years ago,' said Huck dreamily.

'What in the world is the child on about now?' enquired the superintendent.

'We don't listen,' said Jake, 'I'm surprised you still do.'

'Suppose,' said Huck, 'there was a Time Machine, and suppose we all went back on it, would we be better, do you think?' She was frowning and screwing up her eyes with concentration, moving far beyond the walls of the drab office, the sound of distant telephone bells, the hollow, echoing tramp of feet along corridors outside. 'People say it was better in the past. The old man in the gardens thought it would make Jake politer, and it might make Polly want to cook and look after us, and Edward to be a father to us like Felix Underwood in *The Pillars of the House* – that's an old-fashioned book about a huge orphan family in case you didn't know – and . . .'

'And you to be a good obedient little girl who never, never made up stories,' put in Jake.

'Do shut up, Huck,' said Polly, 'other people are in a hurry even if you aren't. So could we have the money?' she asked the superintendent. 'We'll need food.'

'I'm going to give it to Barty, and hope that he has some grasp of practical matters. Here's five pounds, Barty. Buy some chops and fresh vegetables and give them a hot meal. Better still, try to find someone to give you a few cooking lessons.'

'I know,' said Huck, 'why doesn't he get Mr Grant to teach him? Mr Grant does all the cooking while Reg and Mrs Grant look after the shop. Then we could have nice food. We might even,' she said falling into one of her rapt states again, 'have turkey and smoked salmon and pancakes and meringues with cream and turtle soup and oysters and . . .'

'This time I've definitely had enough,' said the superintendent. 'Take her away, someone, will you. You'd better all come back on Monday so I can count you.'

# 5

'I WONDER if I could really ask Mr Grant about cooking?' said Barty, gloomily contemplating the litter of crumbs and paper bags on the kitchen table. They had lunched off Cornish pasties which he had brought back in despair after spending the whole morning staring at hunks of meat. He had inspected every butcher's counter display in the Covered Market six times over, with the hope, that grew all the time fainter, that he might see something which even someone as ignorant as he was instinctively knew how to cook. But it was useless. Supposing he had known what to do with braising steak or New Zealand best end, how could he ask for it when he had no idea what animal it came from, or if it was sold by weight or by numbers?

'Don't bother about cooking now,' said Huck impatiently, 'we've just had lunch. Anyway, Grants' will be shut till two-fifteen. No, what I want you to do,' (she looked over her shoulder secretively to make sure there was nobody within earshot) 'is to draw some dials for the Time Machine.'

'You're not still on about that!' he said wearily.

'Nobody would think you were the one who'd dug it out and brought it home,' Huck raged. 'What did you want to go doing it for if you can't take the slightest interest?'

'What do you want then?'

'I want years and centuries, of course. Shall I tell you what I'm going to do? Well, I've found out that it does work, haven't I, and that I can get back from the day

54

before yesterday, so why don't I try to go back to the real past?'

She looked at Barty triumphantly. He was baffled. He might be a twin brother, but he had never been able to follow her leaps and twists of thought or to work out what she thought was real and what she knew was fantasy. Half the time he suspected she hardly knew herself. 'I thought you didn't like it. I thought you were afraid,' he said at last.

'I was sort of afraid. I mean, I didn't expect it to work, and then it did. It must have, because Mother's passport went *and* you said I disappeared.'

'I only said I thought you did, just for a second, but then you were there again so quickly that it must have been a mistake.'

'So what I want to do,' said Huck, ignoring all this, 'is to try going back really far – beyond last week; after all, I know what happened last week, that's boring. I want to find out what things looked like in the real past. It would really be more fun if it was the future, but we've only got one ivory time handle, and it seems to have made up its mind that it's to go to the past. So you will, won't you? Look, I'll give you the compasses from my geometry set, and I'll tear some paper from my rough book.' She scooped up a satchel from the clutter of shoes and school equipment that had been tossed into the corner of the kitchen, and scrabbled through the contents. 'No, you'd better have the cover of my French vocabulary, the paper's stiffer. And I can't find the compasses, so you'll have to draw round something – I know, one of these mugs.'

'Why can't you draw it?'

'Because you draw the neatest. That's why you're good at geography, I suppose.'

'What do you want me to write?'

'The years, back as far as you can go.'

'There won't be room for many,' said Barty decisively.

Huck reflected. 'No, I suppose there wouldn't. You'll just have to make a selection. Put this year at the top, then don't bother about this century, put 1900 and go backwards from that. Write small, you want to be able to get a lot in. If you can think of years when exciting things happened, put them.'

Barty, having reflected for a moment, decided that he had no views on which were particularly exciting years, and was proceeding backwards in tens. Huck knelt down on a chair beside him and peered over his shoulder. '1890, 1880, 1870 – they all end in nought. Oh, I see what you're doing, you would.'

'And what are our dear little twinnies so busy about?' said Jake's voice behind them.

Huck gave a shriek and folded herself over the piece of paper. 'Go away, it's a secret.'

'And is it connected with the secret you've got locked up in Mother's bedroom, and would that secret be a Time Machine by any chance?'

Huck jumped as though she had been stung. 'How did you know?'

'I didn't, little sister, I was bluffing. But I know now. Besides, you never were able to keep anything to yourself, and though you may not be aware of it, you have been babbling on about the matter fairly freely. Perhaps you would allow me to see it.'

'No,' said Huck violently. 'You go to Wellington Street to your old record shop.'

'Thursday – early closing day, Huck, my love. Well, since Mother's bedroom does not particularly belong to you, I see no reason why I shouldn't look in upon the Machine myself.'

'No!' shouted Huck. She scrambled off her chair,

charged with lowered head at Jake's stomach, and as he staggered back against the doorpost, temporarily winded, she rushed for the stairs. 'Come on, Barty! And bring the dial.'

A few minutes later they were breathlessly trying to hold the bedroom door against the force of Jake on the other side, their feet slipping on the floorboards. Barty struggled with the key. The handle turned and rattled and fists beat on the panels. Huck danced up and down.

'You can't get in. Not unless you get a ladder.'

The hammering stopped. Feet went down the stairs, the front door opened; the house became silent. 'Quick,' said Huck, 'get on with the numbers. You never know with Jake, he may be collecting some of his friends.'

'Sounds as if he's getting a battering ram,' said Barty, standing by the chest of drawers and writing in numbers. Downstairs there was now a heavy bumping as if something was being dragged over the hall floor.

'Then we'll have to pile furniture against the door. He's not going to come in here. Have you nearly finished? It couldn't be Jake, though, he's not coming upstairs.'

'Bo,' said a voice suddenly from just behind them.

The shock was terrifying. Barty gave such a start that the 1820 he was writing swept across the paper and his heart seemed to explode against his ribs. Jake was on the other side of the window. It was hard to see his face against the light, but Barty knew he would be screwing it up into the horrible gargoyle features that were his speciality.

'Fetch a ladder, you said. So being a devoted older brother I borrowed one off a window-cleaner in the road, even though I had to carry it right through the house to get it where I wanted it. And now, said our noble hero, to open the window is the work of a moment.' He began to heave at the lowest sash.

'Don't you dare come in,' shrieked Huck, hurling herself across the room. 'I'll throw the ladder down. I'll chop off your fingers. You're a bullying beast. Lock the window, Barty, and draw the curtains. I'm going to fetch the police. You stay here and guard it.'

But Barty followed her. He couldn't bear to stay there with that shadowy outline faintly visible through the curtains, and the noise of unseen fingers beating a tattoo on the glass. He pulled out the key, slammed the door behind him, locked it on the other side, pushed the key in his pocket and followed Huck.

'Hu – uck,' he called breathlessly down the street as he panted after her. 'Hu – uck.' But the distant figure weaving in and out of the passers-by and dodging the traffic never once looked back. A bus queue in Queen's Street delayed her a little and he drew nearer as she charged down the turning on the other side. As she emerged from the narrow darkness of the lane he put on a furious spurt and caught her up.

'Don't go to the police. Look, Edward's down here somewhere. He might help.'

They were standing now in an open space where every house had been razed, leaving flattened yellow earth scattered with bricks. Not long ago it had been a tight cluster of houses. There was nothing of that left except the narrow streets themselves, thickly crusted with mud from the wheels of the demolition lorries.

'I hate Jake, I hate him, I hate him,' said Huck, sobbing with fury. 'I wish I was a mad bull goring him. I've got a stitch too.' She twisted herself to try to ease it.

'There's Edward.' Barty pointed to a distant group of people crouched on the top of mounds of earth.

'He won't be any good. When have you known Edward

be any good? He might as well not be there for all the good he does.'

All the same she followed Barty. 'Edward,' she called, 'you've got to come. This minute. Jake's bullying. Come and hit him. I don't mind what you do as long as you stop him.'

'Ed, does this belong to you?' said one of the figures squatting on the earth. 'There's someone who seems to have a problem.'

Over the mound was a network of trenches. There was a collection of people, some with trowels, others with sieves, all of them staring up at Huck – all except one who was intently scrutinizing a fragment of pottery. Huck pounced on him.

'You've got to stop Jake. He tried to get through the door first but we locked him out. Then he fetched a ladder and said Bo through the window. It might have killed us, giving us a fright like that. And you've got to stop him getting at the Time Machine.'

Edward, holding the pottery delicately in the palm of his hand, was reluctant even to take his eyes from it for a moment. He glanced up over his glasses. 'Oh, Barty's there, he'll help you, I daresay. But, Huck, I shouldn't hit anybody if I were you.'

'Barty can't help, that's why he's come. We need someone *old*. If you don't come I'm going to fetch the police. And hurry, he'll be breaking up the Time Machine unless we get back quick.'

'What is a Time Machine, a sort of clock?' one of the excavators asked.

Somebody at the bottom of the trench who had been looking earnestly at Huck straightened himself to an upright position. Unlike the others, who were mostly bearded and hairy, he was close-cropped and his face was scrubbed and pink and shining. He was wearing a T-shirt with a large picture of Donald Duck to which was pinned a badge with the dazzle-orange message 'Frodo lives!'

'Of course it's not a clock.' His mild brown eyes looked reproachfully through wire-framed spectacles. 'It's a game. Don't you remember the games you played when you were kids? Don't you remember . . . ?'

'It *isn't* a game,' stormed Huck, 'any more than your silly digging is. This is real. He said Bo to us from a ladder. We might have died from heart attack, some people do. And he's probably wrecking the Time Machine now.'

The excavators were moving over to stare, fascinated. 'Who is this villain?' asked one.

'It's Jake, our brother.'

'What's Jake like, Ed? As black-hearted as his little sister seems to think?'

'He teases,' said Edward, 'I suppose he can be tiresome sometimes.' His mind, however, was not on domestic problems. He picked his way over the earth to one of the team. 'Geoffrey, would you say that this fragment . . .?'

'Teases!' interrupted Huck passionately. 'He blights our lives, that's what he does. An old man this morning said he ought to have gone to an old-fashioned school where they used to beat the boys, and he's right.'

'Borstal, perhaps?' said one.

'They don't beat anybody there any more, though,' said another. He addressed himself to Huck. 'Now if you've got a Time Machine, and it's anything like H. G. Wells's, why don't you take him back a hundred years or so to one of the old public schools?'

'Do you mean like Winchester?' enquired Huck doubtfully. 'We've got school pictures of ancestors who were there, but they look quite happy.'

Edward asserted his authority for once. 'Huck, I think you should go now. You'll probably find that Jake . . .'

Huck ignored him. 'How many years back would I have to take him? We've made a time clock but it only goes to 1830 because that's where Jake interrupted. Is that far enough?'

'You see!' said the Donald Duck character excitedly. 'Isn't it just what I've always been saying about the intensity with which children play? Could you have a better example . . .?'

'*Steve!*' they shouted in exasperation. 'Stow it. Haven't we had enough?'

But Huck was paying no attention. 'What date is best for strictness? I've got to hurry.'

But here an argument broke out between various excavators who had views on the history of education. Some said that what Huck wanted was the early days of the last century when flogging really was flogging, and the headmaster of Eton had personally beaten all the boys in the school in a single morning. Others said that this system only turned boys into brutal young savages and that she would do better to wait until the Victorian reforms had taken hold and the public schools were turning out earnest, high-principled young gentlemen. The discussion got warm, Huck was forgotten.

'Talk, talk, talk, that's all you ever do,' she shouted. 'I suppose I'll just have to try for myself, that's all.'

She slithered from the mound of earth above the trenches and was off. By the time Barty had realized she had gone there was no sign of her. Below him the excavators were settling back to digging up the past. He could hear gusts of laughter and muffled remarks about 'Huxtables'. Hot with shame for Huck, he slunk off. He walked a little way towards the police station, afraid that she might be clamouring at its doors for help, and then on an impulse, turned and hurried home. The door of the house was never locked. As he thrust it open he found Huck standing in the hall with a bland and satisfied face.

'Jake's gone to school,' she announced. 'At least, I suppose he must be nearly there, but I don't know how long coaches take – horse coaches, I mean. And how far is Winchester anyway – I do think you might look a bit more pleased now I've got back.'

'Got back?' said Barty. 'Where from?'

'From 1830, of course. I tell you what, though. Next time I go on the Machine I'm going to take travel sickness pills. It makes you giddy, all those years rushing past you.'

# 6

'THIS house feels queer,' said Polly. She had both hands cupped round her breakfast mug of coffee and was leaning against the sink while she gulped it down. There was not, she said, time to sit; she was already late, and the first pickets should have been on duty half an hour before.

Edward rustled the paper dejectedly. The sports page made dreary reading in March with the cricket season finished in Australia, and the visiting Test Team not yet unshipped in England. 'Where's Jake?' he remarked.

'That's it,' said Polly, 'it's the quiet that's peculiar. He's usually got his record player on by now. When did he come in last night? I didn't hear him.'

Nobody spoke. Barty, crouched at a corner of the table, scrutinizing *Practical Electronics*, tried to bury himself even more deeply in the connecting details of a device for timing your caravan journeys. Polly noticed a certain furtiveness in the movement and pounced. 'Do you know where he is, Barty?'

Lifting his head reluctantly, Barty mumbled, 'He must have got up early. He wasn't in bed when I came down.'

'Not in bed! When have you ever known Jake get up early in the holidays? Ed, do you think we'd better ring the police?'

Edward pulled at his nose. 'Wouldn't they ring us if anything had happened to him?' Then an idea struck him. 'Huck might know something. She was behaving very strangely down at St Botolph's yesterday afternoon and it all seemed to be about Jake.'

63

'Huck's gone out, I know that. She came in to borrow one of my sweaters while I was still in bed – pretty cool, I thought. Then I heard her bang the door.'

Barty, his eyes flickering over the diagrams on the pages by his plate, tried to think what on earth he could say about Jake's whereabouts. All he knew was the confused jumble of hints that Huck had poured out yesterday, and those would hardly reassure anybody. Edward was slowly considering the situation. 'Barty was with Huck when she was making such an exhibition of herself. What was it, Barty? She was shouting something about a Time Machine.'

'It's just something she's made up. A sort of game. Up in Mother's bedroom. And Jake wanted to smash it.'

'I suppose he could be there, then,' Polly said to Edward. 'But if he is, he's keeping very quiet. Not like Jake, really. Come on, we'd better look.'

She shouted up the stairs but nobody came. Striding up, she poked her head into the room that Jake and Barty shared. 'You can't tell if he slept there or not, as he never makes his bed. Where's this Time Machine then? Why, Mother's room's locked!'

'I've got the key,' said Barty uneasily from the hall. 'It was just to keep Jake out.'

'Then I suppose he can't be in. Still, I'm going to have a look and see what Huck *has* been up to. Come on, hand over the key – you'd got no business to take it, anyway. I must say,' (her voice retreated into the bedroom) 'Huck's got a cheek, putting all this junk here. Barty, where are you? Why are you hanging about outside?'

Barty edged his way round the door, and stood just within the threshold. There was something about the Machine that made him uneasy, he didn't want to look at it.

'What an extraordinary thing. Wherever did she find it? And why does she call it a Time Machine anyway?' pursued Polly. 'Oh, I see, there's a clock on the handlebars. Really, I thought she'd have grown out of this sort of game years ago!'

Involuntarily Barty stepped forward a few paces. 'She did get it on then!'

'Get on what?'

'Oh, just this bit of paper,' said Barty warily. The clock-face that he had numbered back to 1830 had now been stuck on the dial. She had had to cut it in half to get it under the hand – a botched-up job; it made him wince to look at it. The 1820 that he had begun to write ended in a pencil stroke right across the dial; it was then that Jake had knocked on the window – the last time, in fact, that he had seen him. Downstairs the front door opened; there was a sound of stampeding footsteps and Huck hurled herself into the room. 'What are you doing here? Get out, all of you. It's mine.'

'I like that!' Polly was indignant. 'It's Mother's room and really, Huck, you can't go bringing all this rubbish in here.'

Huck rounded on Barty. 'What did you go bringing them up here for? You give me that key back, I'm going to keep it. Now everybody's to get out.'

'Nobody's getting out,' said Polly, 'until you tell us where Jake is. Edward seems to think you know. Where've you been, anyway? The library can't be open yet, surely?'

'I went to the chemist,' said Huck sulkily, 'to get some travel sickness pills. It makes you giddy, day and night whizzing past.'

'Huck, just for once talk sense, can you?' said Polly threateningly. 'If nobody knows where Jake is, I'm going to ring the police. He hasn't been seen since yesterday afternoon, and as far as we can make out he didn't come in last night at all.'

'No, he didn't, but I fetched him this morning, early. Then he went out. He said he had a new catapult that he wanted to try.'

'Jake went out early with a catapult?' They were staring at her in amazement when it happened. The front door was thrown open, banged shut, the bolts were drawn and the key turned. They all crowded to the top of the stairs.

'Jake!' Polly strode down into the hall. 'What are you doing and what have you got?'

Huck tugged at Barty's elbow. 'The Time Machine's made him all different,' she said in his ear.

'Different?' Barty peered into the dimness by the front door. It was difficult to see clearly, but it seemed to be the usual Jake standing there, and it was his voice. 'Here, take these, Poll!' he was saying, and Barty saw him thrust two limp objects with dangling necks at her.

Polly recoiled, shuddering. 'Take them away, you know I can't stand dead birds. Where on earth did you get them?'

'From the college lake. There are two of the porters after me now. Poll, old sport, you wouldn't peach on a fellow, would you? Barty, you're a good little chap, you take 'em.'

It looked like Jake who sprang up the stairs towards him, but Jake had never spoken like this, and he had certainly never been known to move quickly. As Barty drew back there was a thundering knock on the door.

'It's those porter johnnies. Quick, Barty, you take the birds, I'll face the music. They can't pin anything on me if the birds are out of the way.'

And so Barty found himself hurtling out of the back

door from the kitchen, clutching the bodies of two mallard. He looked wildly round him; in a garden the size of a tablecloth there were few hiding places. Thomas was stalking along the wall. Seeing an intruder in the garden, which no doubt he expected to have to himself, he gave his tail an irritable twitch and trod on.

It was then that Barty remembered the walls, the network running between the gardens, the thoroughfare of all the cats in the neighbourhood. He had run along them himself when he had been smaller. He stuffed the ducks under his jersey, clambered on to the dustbin and fled.

It was no joke balancing along walls that were full of loose bricks, trying to support two heavy bodies under his sweater. And he had no plan in his head. The wall finished, he knew quite well, where Simon Street joined Wellington Street, and in both cases these were streets of terraced houses, the only way out of their gardens being through their back doors.

It was as he reached the last garden of all, and the backs of the Wellington Street houses were rising up sheer in front of him, that disaster happened. There, a few feet below him, he saw a figure bending over a dustbin. In a fright he stopped, lost his balance and his grip of the ducks. They plummeted on to the wall, from there down beside the dustbin where they sprawled with outspread necks. For a second Barty stared at them in horror, then the wall crumbled beneath him and he crashed down beside them.

'A menace to man and beast,' a voice exploded above his head, 'that's what you boys are nowadays, and I tell you it's the last time I'm having it.' But Barty was too preoccupied with the pain of his banged shin to look up. With eyes shut he clung to his leg and rocked

67

himself backwards and forwards.

'Can't you even answer?' the voice shouted. 'Who are you anyway?'

Barty lifted his head off his knee. He saw a small, fierce, bald man, with ginger moustaches twisted into points, standing with a colander in his hand poised as if he was going to crash it down on Barty's head.

'I know who you are. You're one of them Huxtables. Always up and down this street one or other of you is, making disturbances. And now bringing this wall down. I won't have it, I tell you, and you're coming inside with me while I phone the police. And what's that down there? Ducks? Where did they come from?'

Barty made a grab at the limp feathered bodies. 'Could I put them in your dustbin?'

'I should just about think you couldn't! Stolen property are they? You can bring them in with you and we'll see what the police have to say.'

Barty found himself being propelled through a backyard stacked with empty cardboard cartons, beer crates and boxes, up steps and into the back premises of some unknown house in Wellington Street. It was very dark, and there was a strong smell of firelighters, coal tar soap and rotting brussels sprouts.

'Ern,' shouted a piercing female voice from somewhere beyond the gloom, 'Ern, is that you?'

'You'll have to wait a minute,' said the man to Barty ferociously, 'and don't you leg it, neither. I'll deal with you properly in a minute.' He disappeared into the darkness. 'Just coming, dearie,' he called. The tiger had been suddenly transformed into a dove.

'Ernie, where's those liquorice toffees I took upstairs from the shop yesterday?' said a fretful female voice in the distance. 'A whole pound of them there was which had gone soft. I thought I'd have them for elevenses and now they're lost.'

Suddenly Barty knew where he was – at the back of Grants' shop, and the man with the ginger whiskers must be Mr Grant.

'I'll have a look for them, my dear. I'll be with you in a few moments.'

'I hope you can find them, that's all. I've set my heart on a soft liquorice. Never trust those hard ones, they'd drag every tooth out of your head soon as look at you.'

Mr Grant closed the door on Mrs Grant's voice and pushed Barty roughly up a flight of dark stairs. 'You stay here while I get them. I put them in a clean bag, that's why Mummy couldn't see them.'

When he came back, Barty was standing at the door of a kitchen, staring with awe at the vista of white tiles, stainless steel and glistening surfaces. 'It's like a picture in a magazine!'

Mr Grant's manner softened. 'It's not bad, not for a do-it-yourself job.'

Barty's eyes took in the shelves with the uniform jars of herbs and spices, the cupboards all round the walls, the cooker that glinted with white enamel and steel, and on the table, as if posing for their picture, a couple of fine onions and a bunch of parsley. 'Do you cook like it tells you to do in the Sunday papers?' he asked. 'With wine and things? And garlic – what's garlic?'

Mr Grant shook his head. 'Mummy and Reg can't be doing with that sort of thing, delicate stomachs they've got. No, I stick to the plain. Mind you, I read about it and collect the recipes. And the flavourings too.' He waved his hand towards the jars on his shelves. 'Some chaps collect stamps; I collect them. And these too. Look.' By the cooker was a row of books. 'All the classics,' said Mr Grant proudly, 'Tante Marie, André Simon, Elizabeth David – there's a book club I've joined for them. Some day, maybe, there'll be a chance to do a bit of cordong blue. Till then, there's no harm reading it all up.'

'I want to learn to cook,' said Barty.

'*You?* Where's your mum then?'

'In America. But she doesn't cook much when she's here, she hasn't got time. I'm sick of fish fingers and baked beans. So are we all. We want something hot, with meat in it.'

Mr Grant remembered. 'Ah yes, you're a Huxtable, that's right. Well, there's some that has their careers and some that hasn't. Mummy downstairs, she has her career. I'm glad she does, it gives her an interest. What was it you wanted to cook?'

Barty shook his head hopelessly. 'I looked at the butchers', I thought I'd get some ideas, but it looked so complicated. What to ask for, I mean. And then I wouldn't have known what to do with it.'

'Well,' said Mr Grant slowly. 'I wouldn't mind you coming out shopping with me, once in a way. I could tell you what's value for money, at any rate. But there's those ducks now, what were you thinking of doing with them?'

'The ducks!' Barty looked behind him with horror. He had put them down on a chair by the door and had completely forgotten about them. 'Is there a place in your garden where I could bury them?' he asked urgently. 'It's my brother Jake, he came home with them, and told me to get rid of them. What on earth can I do with them?'

'Wild duck, eh?' Mr Grant surveyed the brown feathers and the tuft of blue on the wings. 'Well, I'll ask no more questions. Was it the canal they came from?'

'The lake at Worcester College,' said Barty warily.

'Ah yes, those college chaps, they wouldn't like that.' Mr Grant went on looking at the ducks, almost wistfully, it seemed. 'There are recipes for wild ducks, you know.'

'Do you mean you can *eat* them?' Barty was as amazed as if he had been told you could put blackbirds into a pie.

'Eat them? Of course you can; game, that's what they are. And the best way of hiding them too – put them in your stomachs. I never thought I'd have the chance of cooking wild duck. Let's look up some recipes. I've got a bit of bacon to boil for their lunch, but that won't take long.'

So Barty sat at the table while Mr Grant thumbed his way through indexes, murmured, considered, and rejected. From time to time he looked uneasily at the mound of feathers by the door and wished that Mr Grant would hurry and make up his mind. At last the decision was made. '*Canard sauvage à la navarraise* – that suit you?'

Barty nodded eagerly. Anything suited him as long as those incriminating feathers disappeared. 'Shut the door then, we'll be putting in garlic, to say nothing of a drop of white wine, and I don't want Mummy to be put off her food by the smell. You any hand at plucking? You'd better have a try while I collect up all the bits and pieces we need.'

Barty would have agreed to pluck an ostrich by this stage; any moment he was expecting angry college porters to come bursting through the door.

It was with a feeling of enormous relief that he saw the trussed bodies in a rich sauce finally deposited in the oven. The earlier stages had been gory and repellent and had been followed by complicated proceedings which Mr Grant had performed with excited enjoyment. The once

71

immaculate kitchen was now afloat with feathers, and there was a welter of the equipment they had used strewed up and down it.

'Now,' said Mr Grant briskly, 'you can help clear up while I start the bacon for lunch.'

Barty was just putting away positively the last knife when he caught sight of the clock. 'It's not half-past twelve! I've got to buy the lunch yet. They did say sausages.'

'Sausages? What, with the duck?'

'Duck?' said Barty in amazement. 'Are we going to eat that?'

'I don't know who else is. Mummy couldn't touch it – besides, what should I say about where they came from? No, you can take them. I'll lend you that dish they're in to carry them.'

It was going to be a perilous journey, Barty thought. First he had to brave Mrs Grant, who would surely want to know why he was carrying a dish out of her shop, strongly scented with the garlic she detested. And then he might easily be stopped in the street by people suspicious of what he was carrying.

But Mrs Grant gave him hardly a glance as he slid past. Her mind had soared far above such as him. 'Stretched from here where I'm sitting to the imperial mints over there,' she was saying. 'The biggest box of chocolates you've ever seen. None of your hard centres either – creams, every mortal one of them.'

He reached home without any more difficulty than you might expect, carrying a hot and heavy two-handled dish through the street, though he had to kick at the door as he hadn't a hand to turn the knob. Somebody wrenched it open and peered out. It was one of Polly's friends, one of the tall, striding High School girls with whom she habitually moved around. The girl (it might have been

Susan, or Caroline, Barty had never been able to sort them out) shouted back over her shoulder.

'It's only your little brother, Poll.'

Polly came down the hall. 'I don't know who we were expecting really, but I daresay there'll be trouble about Jake.'

'The ducks?' said Barty apprehensively.

'Not about those, no. Jake just stood there and said there weren't any ducks on the premises, and the men who had chased him couldn't see any sign of them so they went away. But he's putting on a new act of behaving like something out of *Tom Brown's Schooldays* and rushing round the place like a ten-year-old shooting at people with a peashooter. There are bound to be complaints soon. I must say, I've never known him quite as tiresome as this. What did you do with those ducks, by the way? It was pretty smart the way you disappeared.'

Barty lifted the lid of the enamel dish. A warm rich smell surged out. 'Mr Grant did it. He said to put it in our oven for a bit longer.'

People crowded round. 'Smells a bit of all right,' said somebody. 'We going to have it for lunch?'

'What we need,' said somebody else, 'is French bread and a green salad. And then hey presto, *tout à fait à la francaise*. I'll go and get it, you shove the duck in the oven. Got a bag anybody?' The girl that Barty thought must be Caroline departed.

'Food!' said Huck, sniffing ecstatically as she came downstairs. 'When will it be ready? Not for another quarter of an hour? Barty, I want to show you something.'

She dragged him into the bookroom. She reached up above the grate that was strewn with spent matchsticks and pencil sharpenings, and took down a small picture. 'Do you know who this is?'

73

It was a small pastel drawing that had been there ever since Barty could remember, a picture of a boy of fourteen or fifteen lolling in a chair with a couple of dead rabbits at his feet. It was always known in the family as 'Charles James Huxtable, born 1815' because this was what was written on the back in faded ink. Huck used to make up long stories about why the dead rabbits were there, and people had from time to time remarked that there was a strong family resemblance between this boy and Jake.

'Of course I do.'

'I bet you don't then.' Huck looked half triumphant, half scared. 'I think I've gone and turned Jake into him.'

If she had expected Barty to react with great surprise to this announcement, then she must have been disappointed. The family was so used to Huck's extravagant romancing that they brushed it aside without even listening to it properly. The surprising thing about this one, if Barty had been in a mood to notice, was that Huck seemed almost frightened by it. But Barty's mind was on the ducks. Nothing like them had ever been eaten in this house. Would they all like them? The responsibility weighed upon him. He was also getting very hungry and trying to work out how long it would take Caroline to reach the shops.

'Oh, do look round,' Huck was complaining. 'It's awful talking to somebody's back. You don't seem to realize how important this is. I was telling you about it yesterday, but you weren't listening then.'

Barty turned back from the window where he had been peering down the street to see whether by any chance Caroline was returning. He looked blankly at Huck. 'Has Jake been getting into trouble again, then?'

'You don't seem to notice anything,' Huck stormed.

'You're as bad as Edward – worse. Always thinking about stupid gadgets to make doors open without people and not seeing the things that are really happening. Can't you see how different Jake is?'

Barty thought about it. 'He's talking differently, but then he gets moods of imitating different plays he's seen. He just does it to tease. And I suppose it was queer him going out and taking those ducks – but it's probably all part of the act.'

'It isn't an act,' said Huck mysteriously. 'It's the Time Machine. I told you about taking him on it yesterday, didn't I?'

Barty was on surer ground now. 'I didn't understand what you were on about yesterday. You kept on babbling about the Time Machine and how it made you sick and Jake felt sick and you'd left Jake somewhere and you didn't know how long to leave him because you didn't understand how long time was in the past. It was all such a muddle nobody could have understood.'

'I still don't understand how long time was in the past,' said Huck musingly. 'That part of the hymn, "A thousand ages in thy sight are as an evening past", I never could work it out. So I didn't know how long in *our* time a year of Jake's time would be. And besides, the way you've made the Time Machine clock it measures ten years at a time, so it was all very difficult. Still, I managed,' she said complacently.

But Barty had heard the front door opening. 'There she is,' he said, escaping into the hall.

It was not Caroline. Jake stood there, clutching a jacket that bulged strangely. 'That's a good smell inside. You haven't gone and polished off all the grub, though, have you, you greedy vagabonds?'

# 7

'You see what I mean about Jake,' Huck was saying. Now that lunch was over and Thomas was delicately licking the last tastes of duck from the bones that had been thrown out in the garden, she had Barty pinned in the bookroom again.

Jake had certainly been very tiresome at lunch. He had sprawled all over the table, flicking bread pellets at the girls, whom he had monotonously teased. And it had not been his usual elegant badinage, either, but crude remarks about sisters who nagged and fussed and spoilt a fellow's fun, all interspersed with sly tweaks at Polly's hair. Caroline and Susan, eyeing him with disdain, had removed themselves as soon as the meal was over, and Polly had stayed only long enough to remind Barty to lay in some supper, and to hope savagely that Jake would have come to his senses before she next saw him. It had been Barty who had, single-handed, cleared the table and washed up, idly watched by Jake (who made witless jokes about fellows who did women's work), and by Huck who was jumping from foot to foot and impatiently urging him to hurry.

By the time Barty had thrown down the sodden tea-towel and had followed her into the bookroom he had had enough. He felt as if he had spent all day cleaning up kitchens, and as it appeared that the family now accepted he was their housekeeper there seemed to be no reason why he should not go on drudging for the rest of the holidays.

'He spoilt everything,' said Barty with indignation.

'Nobody even noticed the food, and it took all morning, and you should have seen the feathers and stuff I had to clear up and bury in Mr Grant's backyard.'

'Still, he did bring the ducks. I suppose that Charles James Huxtable must have gone in for shooting at things, that's why there are those dead rabbits in the picture.'

'You keep on talking about that picture.'

'And every time I talk you won't listen. I thought I'd never get you to stop pottering round out there.'

'Go on then.' Barty grumpily flung himself down in a chair.

Huck paced the rug in front of the fireplace. 'Of course the trouble with the Machine is that it doesn't travel in Space. Only in Time. So you finish up exactly where you started. But luckily I realized, so I knew just where I was when I got there.'

'Got where?'

'Back to 1830. I've told you enough times. All right, I'll tell you again, but listen, will you? It was yesterday – you remember about yesterday, don't you? We went down to the digging – Jake had been awful – and they talked about schools.'

'Yes, I remember. They all thought you were off your nut, and I don't blame them.'

Huck ignored this. 'So I thought the farther back the better, because the schools would be stricter then. I mean, everybody always says when *they* were children how strict things were, and it was worse with their grandfathers, and so . . .'

'Oh, come *on*,' said Barty wearily. 'Tell what happened to Jake, not what you thought.'

'I'd tell you if you didn't keep stopping me. So I ran back from St Botolph's and I found Jake in the garden. He'd got a knife and he said somebody had just told him that it was quite easy to open the catch of a window; you could put a knife between the panes. So he went up the ladder and got into Mother's room and I went in after him. I said if he'd like to try the Machine I would sit on the saddle and he could stand over the crystal bar. I put on the dial that you'd made; it was difficult, I had to cut it in half and find glue. You had some in your bedroom. Then I pushed the hand back to 1830, and moved the crocodile handle, and then the days and nights started whizzing. They went terribly fast, it was like very fast cars driving past you in the dark; you got all dazzled and you had to shut your eyes. Also, there were great whooshes of hot and cold sometimes – I suppose that was summers and winters.'

'Was Jake still there?' Barty, as so often happened, was being swept up into Huck's story in spite of himself.

'He was falling about and yelling about feeling sick. I told him to hold on to the handlebars or he'd get lost in some year that I didn't know about and I'd never be able to find him again. It seemed to go on for ages. I thought something might have gone wrong with the Machine and we'd land up when there were dinosaurs. Anyway, suddenly it stopped, and there we were in Mother's bedroom again.'

'What, just the same place?'

'The same room, but different *time* – I've told you all that. Of course it would have been much better if there was a steering wheel or something to take you to a different place, it would save a lot of trouble. As a matter of fact, I think this house must just have been built then. It had that buildery sort of smell about it, and it was all empty and bare and dirt all over the floor and no glass in the window.'

'Was Jake there?'

'Yes, but it wasn't Jake, I could tell that the minute I looked at him. It was Charles James Huxtable, and wearing just the same clothes as he does in that picture. But he seemed to know me, though, so I suppose,' said Huck complacently, 'that he must have had a sister just like me. He was saying that we'd have to run because he'd heard the church clock strike ten and that he'd told Papa (that's what he said) that he'd be back by ten to set off for the coach. So we ran down the stairs. There were lots of wood shavings everywhere and a nice smell of wood, and somebody was banging with a hammer in a downstairs room. The man who was banging came out to see us. I remember what he wore, too. It was a long white apron with a big pocket on the front, and a funny hat which looked as if it had been folded out of paper. And he said, "Are you off now, young master?" and Jake said, "I'll be back again at the end of the half," and the man said he was sorry there wouldn't be any more larking about as all the houses in this street would be finished by then and have curtains up and people living in them. He was right, too.'

'How do you mean?'

Huck waved her hand impatiently. 'I'll come to that. So we went out into the muddy road, and there wasn't a pavement and it was all muddy and churned up and there were a few horses and carts standing around, and scaffolding and men carrying bricks. And Jake dragged me along and I kept tripping because the road was so rough. Just round the corner we got to a cobbled street. There was a white house in it with a brass door knocker and a little garden with a white fence. (I know that house, it's called Prospect House and it's in Beaumont Street, only it hasn't got a fence now and it's all tidied up and paved in front.) As a matter of fact I think we've got a drawing of it somewhere. I think it's in the album under the sofa.'

'Don't look for it now, for heaven's sake.'

'Well, I'm sure it's there somewhere. Where did I get to? Oh, yes. Jake (or Charles James, whatever you like to call him) marched up to the door of Prospect House and banged on it, and a maid person who called him Master Jem came and opened it and said something about the whole place being topsy turvy looking for him and what a state he was in with dust all over his clothes. Then there seemed to be a lot of people brushing him and putting him into a very tight overcoat with velvet round the collar. They were so busy they didn't notice me. And a tall man came out on the steps and said it was a disgrace, he couldn't be trusted for a minute and they would have to walk very fast if the coach wasn't to go without him. So we did walk fast. It would have been very interesting to see what things have changed now in the streets, but the trouble was I couldn't look much because I was running to keep up.'

'Where were you going to, the railway station?'

'Of course it wasn't the railway station, it was miles before railways. We went to somewhere called the Golden Cross. It's still there, isn't it? There was a yard and such a smell of horses you can't think. You know that Linda Hersey at my school? She's so gone on horses that she sits and snuffs at some old duster that they polish horses with because she says it smells so good. We sing "Horsey Hersey, don't you stop, you let your hooves go clippety clop . . ."'

'Oh, do get *on*,' said Barty crossly. 'You've been telling this story for hours.'

'It's your fault, you keep interrupting. Well, in this yard there was a coach with horses stamping around and boys sitting on the top making a frightful row and blowing things. (Don't you remember me telling you?) They were peashooters and one of the peas hit me and I shrieked. Jake said I was a muff to shriek. (Yes, he did call me a muff, I remember distinctly.) I pushed my head in his stomach and the tall man, Papa (I suppose he was my father, too), pulled me away and said I was a shameless hoyden and when was I going to behave like a lady. Then Jake climbed up and sat on top and somebody blew a horn, and the boys seemed to have little horns and they blew them too. And the coach went away.'

'Where was it going to?'

'To Winchester. Taking the boys back to school. Jake (or Charles James) must have had other friends living here who went too.'

'But how do you *know* they were going there?'

'Jake has turned into Charles James, hasn't he? And Charles James went to Winchester, we all know that, we've got the school roll with his name on in Latin – Carolus Jacobus Huxtable,' said Huck, with the sort of patience that she might have used to an extremely old grandparent.

'Why should he have turned into that boy, why couldn't he have turned into millions of other boys in 1830 or wherever it was you say you took him?'

'I don't know *why*, any more than you do,' said Huck irritably. 'You ask so many questions; why can't you just listen?'

Barty grew heated. 'I like that. If I say nothing then *you* say I'm not taking any notice, and if I ask questions then you complain.'

'You ask such stupid questions, wanting reasons for everything. As a matter of fact, I do know why it's Charles James Huxtable that he's turned into, it's because the Time Machine only works inside this family, and don't you go asking why that is or I'll . . . Now who's that at the door? It's too quiet to be the police or Lucy Soper.'

A moment later she was back. 'It's a little man with

81

ginger whiskers,' she said in a loud whisper. 'He says he wants you. Who is he?'

Barty went out into the hall. Mr Grant was standing on the doorstep with a plastic carrier bag. 'My word, that front door of yours could do with a bit of paint, couldn't it? I was just passing on my way to the Market and I thought that if you wanted to come too I could show you your way round, like, and help you choose a bit of meat.' His manner seemed somehow halting and hesitant.

Huck came up behind Barty and stared at him. 'Are you Mr Grant? Did you cook that duck?'

'It was partly that that I came about,' said Mr Grant, brightening. 'Not to put too fine a point upon it, I did wonder how it was, not having ever tried anything in the cordong blue manner before.'

'It was *beautiful*,' said Huck dreamily. 'Real food. It tasted. You know how most food doesn't really taste. Can you teach him some more?'

Mr Grant glowed. 'I thought that with what we put into it it wasn't going to be an outright failure, but I wanted to hear firsthand.'

'What other things can you show us how to do?' demanded Huck.

'There's any amount. Your brother's seen the books – you name it, I've got it,' said Mr Grant proudly. 'The first thing is, how's your kitchen equipped?'

'Well,' said Barty, hesitating dubiously as he remembered the gleam and precision that Mr Grant was used to. But Huck burst out.

'It's just been cleared up. And we've got a super cooker. The other one was so old, it back-fired or something and scorched Mrs B's wig (she was our last cleaning lady and she collected wigs). So Mother told her to go and buy a new one (and she did, it was bright red) and a new cooker for us, and she chose the most expensive one she could find in the gas showrooms. Only no one's ever used it properly. Mother once lit the oven to warm something up, and we couldn't think what the awful smell was, and then we found it was the book of instructions that she'd left inside. There were some good recipes in it too.'

'Perhaps we could just have a look at it then. I mean, it's not much good us starting to make soufflés, is it, if it turns out you haven't got any soufflé dish or egg whisk.'

'I don't know if we've got things like that,' said Barty dismayed, 'we just don't do cooking at all really.'

But Mr Grant was already stumping down the passage in the wake of Huck. 'There,' she said, flinging the door open. 'Oh, Jake's here, but don't worry about him.'

Jake was indeed there, sitting at the table. He had eaten a large meal only half an hour before but he had now surrounded himself with every jar the larder possessed, from pickles to plum jam, which he was smearing liberally on the hunks that he had cut from the loaf in front of him. Mr Grant rested his carrier bag on the table and stared round, amazed.

'Well, my word,' he said at last. 'Well, I never did.' He shook his head and went on staring.

'Jake's untidied it all again,' said Huck crossly. 'We did clear the table, honestly.'

'Untidy!' For a moment words failed Mr Grant. 'It's like a blooming rubbish dump after a herd of bulls has been rampaging through it. Mad bulls,' he added. 'Doesn't ever anybody pick things up in this place?' He nodded towards the newspapers and library books and paper bags that were lying on the floor, the satchels and school coats, the saucers of cat food and the milk bottles.

'I do,' said Barty. 'But then people come in and make it untidy again.'

'It's not a job for you single-handed,' exploded Mr Grant. 'It's for all of them to help you. Look at the mess you've made, for one,' he roared at Jake. 'And what about the girls, you've got a big sister, haven't you, where's she?'

'That's right, where's she?' Jake stood up. 'What are sisters for, I'd like to know. Anyway, I'm going now. Might come back with some feathered friends.' He laid one finger by the side of his nose, winked at Barty, pulled what looked like a catapult out of his pocket and was off.

'Was that the one that got the ducks?' said Mr Grant grimly. 'Well, you can tell him from me that they used to hang people for less than that. And I'll tell you another thing, I'm not lending a hand with any cooking here, that's for sure!'

'But how can we learn if we're not taught?' Huck was outraged. 'Somebody's got to teach us or we'll starve before Mother comes home.'

'If you feel like that about it, then you'd better set to and make this place more like a kitchen. Nobody could cook here and nobody ought to; they'd die of food poisoning on the spot. To say nothing of there isn't even room to put a knife down on the table. But the real person who ought to be ashamed of herself is that sister of yours, and you can tell her so from me. You get this muck cleared up and then I'll think about helping you a bit.'

As the front door closed behind Mr Grant, Huck and Barty stared at each other.

'It's Jake's fault,' said Huck furiously. 'It was all tidy, and then he has to sit down and start eating again. Look at it all.' She gave the table a kick. 'Look at the sticky stuff he's spread all over the table, and he didn't even bother to put a plate down either!'

But Barty's anger for once outdid Huck's. 'It's not just Jake, it's everybody.' He struggled for words. 'As fast as I clear up, they mess everything again. Nobody cares except me. Why should I have to do it all? Polly and her lot ate that food and didn't even say thank you, and I suppose she'll be bringing them back and they'll expect more food. Well, I'm going down to the prison if that's where they are and I'll tell them what Mr Grant said, and I'll tell them no more food.'

'Wait, I'm coming too.' Huck went to pick up a coat from the heap in the corner and let out a screech. '*He's* done it! I saw him come in with a bulge under his jacket and I suppose he hopes that I'll be blamed. Well, if you want more proof that he's Charles James Huxtable, there it is.'

Barty, peering over her shoulder, saw two dead rabbits.

# 8

WHEN Barty and Huck flung themselves out of the house a moment or so later, they were frantic with anger. Huck was trying to scramble into her coat as she ran, floundering over her long skirt without a hand available to hitch it up, muttering, cursing; Barty was mouthing incoherent phrases – 'It's not fair,' 'Why should it always be me?' These lacked punch, he knew, and this maddened him more.

They were heading towards the prison, where Polly and her friends would presumably be patrolling in their self-imposed task of rousing apathetic public opinion against the jailers and for the prisoners. They had navigated the queues that trailed in the bus station waiting for transport home after the Friday shopping, when Huck suddenly pulled up outside a coffee house. Called Bucking Beans, it was popular with undergraduates. She banged on the window and made threatening gestures.

'Is Polly in there?' Barty, who had nearly fallen over her, pressed his nose against the pane.

'Those people from St Botolph's are; I'm going in to tell them about Jake.'

The boiling fury inside Barty sank a little, and a chilly foreboding took its place. With Huck in this state of mind he never knew what she might say. He tried to pull her back. 'They'll think you're nuts. They already do.'

It was too late, she was pushing her way inside, into a warmth heavy with the smell of coffee, thick with cigarette smoke, and pulsing with guitar. The excavators, sprawled on their elbows among dirty coffee cups, did not have a chance; Huck was on them like an avenging fury. Barty's premonitions about what she might say in her passion were well-founded; a torrent of accusations came pouring out, about Time Machines, schools, Jake, people who read books but didn't know anything about history, all competing with a husky disembodied voice which asserted 'Betcha by golly, wow' somewhere in the region of the ceiling.

Huck's voice won. The occupants of adjacent tables screwed themselves round to stare at her and at the St Botolph's party slumped, defeated.

'OK, OK,' said one of them feebly at last. 'So we don't understand about Time, and someone called Jake has gone to the wrong school in the wrong year. Do you want us to say sorry, or what?'

'You can say sorry till you're purple, but it won't be any good now. One of you said 1830 was a good year to send my brother Jake to school in, to get him to behave better, but it's made him far worse – greedy, rude, silly, and he shoots at rabbits and pretends I did it.'

Light dawned on one member of the party. 'Did you say 1830?'

'That's where I took him. I thought the earlier I took him the more they'd beat him.'

'But you made a mistake, you see. Beating doesn't tame people, it turns them savager. Anyway, the schools were like bearpits in those days, the boys fought the masters, and poached, and got drunk, and bullied . . .'

'He bullies. He hasn't got drunk yet. What can I do?'

'Get out of here, for one thing.'

'Do about Jake, of course.'

A man stood up. 'There's Steve outside. Bring him in.'

'Steve!' said another. 'You want him! You must be

mad, when it's taken us all this time to shake him off!'

'Didn't he say that one of the books he wanted to write was about child psychology? Maybe he can apply it here.'

There was no need to fetch him, Steve had come in. He was shambling in a pair of canvas shoes that were four sizes too large for him and were secured, in the absence of laces, by safety pins. A jacket with 'Albuquerque Tigers' written on it partially covered Donald Duck, and his mild, brown, dog-like eyes beamed with pleasure; you could almost see him wagging a tail. 'Thought I'd lost you guys – been up and down the place looking.'

'We've got a job for you.'

Steve wagged more than ever. 'Yea?'

'Take this kid off our hands. She's Edward Huxtable's sister. He doesn't seem to be around, and she's as crazy as they come. Just up your street.'

'Uh huh?' Steve stared at Huck with deep interest. 'Now if she's what they call psychotic I don't know that I'm your man. There are some who'd take her on, of course. You see the difference between psychosis and . . .'

The groans that went up from the excavators did not muffle Huck. 'He's American. He won't know anything about English schools.' She turned her back on Steve. 'What I want to know is what to do about Jake, and it's your job to tell me. It's because of what you said that he's like this.'

'How about the influence of a good woman, sisterly devotion and all that? Not you, get your sister Polly on to him and get her quick. Say we sent you, if you like, but get out before you're thrown.'

'Time Machine her!' called one of the party as Huck stalked past the tables. 'Turn her into a nice Victorian

grown-up sister – they had a way with brothers, and a
firm hand with their little sisters too.'

'The police would bless you. She had her teeth into
another one today!'

Barty tried to catch her up outside. 'You mustn't go on
like that. It makes you sound crazy.'

'I'll talk how I like,' Huck yelled back over her shoulder, and charged on.

The prison was a building that looked rather like a
toy fort. It had little towers and battlements and a
large entrance gate studded with nails. Steps led into it,
lined with iron railings, and against these leaned a straggling group of girls, the banners that had once been
stretched between them now trailed limply on the pavement. Everybody looked cold and disheartened; their
hair blew across their faces, their hands were stuffed in
coat pockets. Huck rushed up to the shabbiest of them.

'Polly, you're to come home this minute. You're going
to come home and tidy up the kitchen – that's what I
say and Barty says. We can't be doing everything always.
Mr Grant says you ought to be ashamed of yourself. And
you've got to do something about Jake – that's what
Edward's friends say.'

Some of the girls seemed embarrassed, some giggled.
The bored policeman by the prison gate grinned offen-
sively. 'Family life catching up on you, eh?'

'Really, Huck, you've got a nerve,' said Polly furiously.

'Mr Grant says he's not going to do anything about
showing us how to cook until you start helping. And
Jake's put some dead rabbits into the kitchen. Anyway,
you aren't doing anything here.'

'She's right, you know,' said the policeman. 'Count
yourself lucky that you can get a cup of tea. But you're
the privileged sex.'

Polly walked home in a towering rage. On the other

hand, Huck's rage seemed to have abated. In fact, she smirked and giggled as though she was enjoying some sort of private joke, giving Barty sidelong glances, and then quickly looking away again. 'I've had an idea,' she said when they reached Simon Street, 'only I'm not telling you because you'd say I wasn't to.'

Barty could tell from Polly's back how angry she was. She flung open the front door so that the knob crashed against the wall and then turned on Huck. 'I wasn't going to say anything in the street, but I'll say it now.'

Huck did not trouble to reply. She picked up her flowing skirts and tore upstairs, fumbled somewhere down her dress for a key, and let herself into her mother's room. Polly was after her.

'And you're not going to get away like that!'

The door slammed. Barty could hear their voices, then there was silence. For a moment he stood there irresolute, then he wandered into the bookroom, switched on the electric fire and crouched on the hearthrug with the *Guinness Book of Records*.

One person's feet came downstairs. He was aware that somebody had looked in at him from the doorway and had then gone on to the kitchen, but he kept his eyes stubbornly on the page. After a bit he gave up all pretence of interest in the facts in front of him and sat up and listened. He went out into the hall. Nobody was moving. 'Huck?' he called experimentally.

'I'm here if you must know.'

When he went into the kitchen to look for her, she was sitting at the table with a hunk of bread and treacle in front of her. He could see at a glance that she was cross.

'If you were any good you could work it out for me.'

'Work out what?' Barty said in amazement.

'How long Polly will have to be left in 1870 before I bring her back.'

'I don't know what on earth you're talking about. Where is she, anyway? She seemed to be in a flaming temper and now she's quiet.'

'I told you where she was. But what I don't know is how time passes in the past when we're in the present. I mean, there's Polly in 1870 and here's us now. If I leave her for half an hour in our time, how long will it have been in her time?' Huck was restless and uneasy; she had only nibbled at her bread and treacle and was staring at the red hand of the kitchen clock as it sped through the seconds. 'It needs someone who's good at maths. Why can't you do it? Why don't you *say* something – just standing there and staring!'

'You managed with Jake, or you said you did anyway,' said Barty with an effort. 'What did you do then?'

'I left him for a whole night. I didn't know how long it meant he was away at school because I never asked, but look what it did to him! As a matter of fact, I think it's because of your dial; I mean, it only goes back in tens, how can you get things right that way?'

Barty was incensed. 'I was only doing what you told me!'

'Tens is not good enough,' said Huck moodily. 'Just one year makes a difference to people. I got Jake back to the wrong date, I'm sure I did. He seems to have come back so much younger, haven't you noticed?'

'He still looks the same.'

'I'm not talking about what he *looks* like.' Huck was contemptuous. 'I'm talking about the way he acts. I think the Machine got back earlier than 1830 and caught Charles James Huxtable when he was thirteen or something. So I'm wondering now about Polly, she may come back younger or she may be older. I'm just hoping I'll be able to find her easily. I was lucky about Jake.'

'How do you mean, lucky?'

'I might have had to go all the way to Winchester to fetch him, mightn't I? But I found him in the street, playing.'

'I don't know what you're talking about,' said Barty wearily.

'All right then, I'll tell you. You remember what I told you about me seeing him off on a coach with other boys? I just don't know how long he spent at school then, but it was a whole evening of our time (we played Flying Demon, don't you remember?) and a whole night. Then I woke up early, before anybody else was up, and I dressed and went to the Time Machine. It was difficult about the hand, I told you that, but I hoped I had made it a later date than the one I had taken him back to. And it was too,' she said triumphantly. 'Because the first time there had been builders in this house; now it had people and furniture.'

'What on earth did the people say when you turned up?'

'Oh, there weren't any in the room. But somebody came into the hall when I was going downstairs and said 'It's one of those Huxtables again.'' I went out into the street, and there was Jake running, banging at people's knockers and throwing things through the area gratings. I said he'd got to come, and he said he wanted to throw more squibs but the ones he'd got were damp and wouldn't bang and he hadn't got any tin to buy more. (I've looked up "tin" in the Slang Dictionary and it's old-fashioned for "money".)'

'Was he wearing old-fashioned clothes?'

Huck screwed up her eyes. 'Yes, he was, like in the picture. But he didn't look funny, he looked right. And I suppose I was, because nobody seemed to think I was wrong. Everything felt quite natural, as if I'd always been there, really. Perhaps I belong to then and not to now. Perhaps it's only a ghost of me you're seeing now.'

'Don't,' said Barty. 'You make me feel giddy.'

'So do you think,' (Huck's eyes had returned to the kitchen clock) 'that I ought to go and fetch her now? She's had ten minutes of our time. I suppose it doesn't make any difference, really. The past has happened; nothing in our time can change that, it's just a question of getting the time dial right. Why can't you be thinking about that, instead of reading those stupid things about how deep the deepest diver has ever been – which you must know by heart anyway as it's the only book you read?'

'I know one thing. You're very cross.'

'So would you be, trying to find someone with a Time Machine that doesn't work properly. All right then, I'll go now.'

Barty heard her stumping upstairs. He was puzzled; uneasy too. Huck was usually so calmly confident about her plans; this doubting, anxious mood was entirely new. He hovered at the bottom of the stairs, peering up at the closed door of their mother's room. Footsteps ran across the floor; Huck pulled open the door, banged it behind her. 'She's there,' she called down to Barty in a low voice, 'and she's in a foul temper, I can tell you. Look out, she's here.'

Polly came treading down towards them, though at first he hardly recognized her, so different was her hair from the usual fair mane that kept flopping round her face. Now she had taken it up, plaited it, and wound it round her head. She was carrying a bundle of leaflets.

'Really, I don't know why you have to stare like that. And will you let me get past?'

'It's just your hair,' Barty said lamely.

'Personal remarks are very ill-mannered, surely you know that.' She pushed her way past the pegs where such coats as were not tossed on the floor hung by the front door.

'Are you going *out*?' demanded Huck.

'Certainly I am going out.'

'But you've got to stay and tidy the kitchen!' Huck's voice was shrill with indignation. 'Mr Grant says. So do Barty and I. I *told* you that was what we wanted.'

There was quite as much indignation in Polly's voice. 'Help in the kitchen – when there are all those hungry minds in the streets of the city! And you know that Friday is my district visiting night. Don't touch those pamphlets, I've been all afternoon putting them in order.'

It was too late, Huck had picked up the bundle that Polly had put down on the stairs. The elastic band that held them together snapped and a cascade of paper poured on the floor. Barty had seen them before, little paper-covered leaflets printed on cheap paper now brittle with age and marked with brown spots, which some bygone Huxtable had apparently used for distributing among the poor : advice on how to save money, on how servants should behave, on the evils of smoking and drinking. *Cleanliness is Next to Godliness* said one with a picture of a woman bending over a washing tub. *Tim Clod – Furnaceman* said another showing a beery brute puffing at a huge pipe. *Mother's Ruin* said a third over a bottle labelled GIN. Huck made no attempt to pick them up, she just squatted there and stared.

'What on earth are you going to do with them?' she said to the furious Polly.

'When they are picked up, they are going to be distributed in Wellington Street. And will you hurry, please; my time is precious, if yours is not.'

'To Wellington Street?' echoed Barty.

'To Wellington Street certainly, it is a notorious area, even in this district.'

# 9

BARTY had locked himself in the bedroom when Jake came hammering at the door. Though they shared the room, it was stamped with Jake's personality. The black walls were stuck with gigantic colour cut-outs of Cinzano and Dubonnet bottles, and blown-up photographs of death-masks between whose waxen lips Jake had put sometimes a pipe, sometimes a cigar. There were plastic skulls with candles in them here and there, and a small stuffed alligator spun languidly on a thread above his bed. A battery of spotlights was focused on the drums, and there was a strong smell of joss stick. Two or three model planes, and a neat pile of *Practical Electronics* identified it as a room in which Barty also had a bed.

'Open the door, can't you?' bawled Jake from outside. 'I've just about had enough of girls.'

Reluctantly Barty pushed away the notebook into which he had been copying diagrams. Ruling the lines, numbering and lettering them was soothing and absorbing; it was a remedy he had hardly ever known to fail. He went over to the door, which was now being kicked irritably, and peered out.

'You might let a fellow in,' grumbled Jake, pushing through. 'I want to get away from her just as much as you.'

'Who? Polly?'

'Oh, her too, but she's out now. No, little sisters – always yapping and screeching. Look at that, she's here now.'

Huck's head had appeared on the stairs. 'There you

are, Barty. Why didn't you answer when I called? I shouted and shouted. I've got something to show you.'

'Later, I've got something I want to finish.' Barty tried to retreat.

'Just one of your machines. It can wait. This is important.'

Huck won. She always did when it came to a battle of wills. Full of foreboding he followed her down into the bookroom. She climbed on to a chair and pointed to a photograph on the wall. 'Look at that.'

'I can't see, you're in the light.'

'All right, I'll get it down.'

She unhooked it and handed it to him. He knew it, though he had never bothered to look at it closely before, dismissing it as yet another bit of lumber that the family had held on to for generations. He found himself staring at a collection of young girls sitting on somebody's lawn in smothering clothes. Their feet stuck out straight in front of them, their anxious little faces were nearly extinguished under huge hats that surely must have been borrowed from their mothers. In the centre, as upright as a lamp-post, with an expression on her face that threatened doom to any fidgety child, was Polly – the new Polly, with her hair parted in the middle and tightly wound round her head. 'Mary and her sewing class, 1870', somebody had written underneath.

'I know where that photograph was taken,' said Huck triumphantly, 'it was Fyfield Road. And do you know how I know? Because I went there and saw those girls! Well, don't stare at me like that; it makes you look like that mad girl in the film – the X one that the cinema manager turned me out of. Don't you want to hear what happened? I've been trying to find out for ages to tell you, and Jake won't listen. I suddenly saw that photograph just now and everything fitted in. You know how

Polly came back with us from the prison?'

Barty did remember. He also remembered the extraordinary hush that fell on the house after she had followed Huck upstairs.

'She rushed into Mother's bedroom and I sat down on the Time Machine. She came behind and grabbed my shoulders – I think she was going to shake me, but she didn't have time because I started the machine and then she had to hold on to stop falling off. I had taken a travel pill, but I still felt giddy because I don't think I had taken it early enough. But Polly must have felt awful. I had put the hand of the dial to 1870 – I don't know why, it must have been inspiration. And then, there we were in Mother's bedroom. Only it was all furnished quite differently of course, it looked much nicer than it does now, the wallpaper had pretty flowers on it and there were lots of pictures and white curtains tied back with bows. And the bed was all draped in white and there was this girl lying in it.'

'What girl?'

'How should I know? Somebody ill, and Polly had come to see her. Polly talked to her in a lectury sort of way and gave her a little book or something, and then we went out. That was when I knew that it wasn't our house. We walked up Simon Street. The funny thing was, it was just like it had been with Jake. It didn't feel that what I was doing was strange. You know how you do extraordinary, mad things in dreams and it all seems right? It was like that. So I seemed to know where we were going even though it must have been different.'

'How do you mean, different?'

'Because it was a hundred years ago, of course,' said Huck impatiently. 'Over a hundred years. You're supposed to be good at maths. Take 1870 from . . .'

'All right, all right,' said Barty.

'Don't keep interrupting, then. So then we got to Fyfield Road. I knew it was Fyfield Road, just knew, and anyway, the name was written up on the wall. It was the house near the corner, with steps up and a door that looks like the entrance to a church. And it was our house, I mean, our house then.'

'How did you know?'

'Anybody can feel whether it's their own house, can't they? Besides, Polly behaved as though it was. She marched up the steps and pulled a brass knob, which made a bell jangle inside, and a maid in a frilly cap let us in. We went into a room with a big table covered with sewing things, and Polly started pinning and cutting. Then she said, "Don't just stand there looking, fetch your hemming." I told her that she wasn't going to get me to do any sewing, and I went. It was like in a dream you sometimes tell yourself to wake up. Only this wasn't a dream.'

'How did you wake up then?'

'I tell you,' said Huck indignantly, 'it wasn't a dream. I went back to the house – this house – where I'd left the Time Machine in the girl's bedroom. I don't think she could see it; it must be invisible to everybody but me when it gets to the past. I told somebody at the door that I'd left a book behind, and went upstairs and came home. Now shall I tell you how I found Polly again?'

'No,' said Barty, standing up and trying to get past her.

'I'm going to. It was quite easy, because I knew where to go when I left this house. I ran to Fyfield Road, and there was Polly with a whole lot of girls about my age, sitting in the back garden sewing. I could hear their voices, so I just went through a garden gate and found them. And it's that garden in the photograph, the same conservatory, the same french window and steps coming down – everything. I just said to Polly, "That girl in Simon Street is calling for you", and she came straight away. And I brought her back. It's strange, though,' said Huck brooding, 'how the Time Machine turns us into our ancestors. And the Huxtables seem to have been so horrible. Now, if I could find a really nice one I could make Edward into him. Or you.' She suddenly turned on Barty and fixed a long, considering look on him.

'No!' shouted Barty. 'Don't look at me like that. Stop it! Those St Botolph's people are right, you're crazy!'

It was nearly dark when he rushed outside; a fine drizzle was falling. He had no idea where he was running, he just wanted to put as much distance as he could between himself and Huck. That was what witches must look like, or hypnotists. If he stayed with her a minute longer he felt he might himself have some spell put on him. When lack of breath made him slow down he was near the middle of the town. The shops had closed now, the streets had emptied except for a few bunches of people who were straggling apathetically into the cinema which advertised *I Was a Teenage Virgin from Outer Space*.

'Hey there!' called somebody. 'Hey there, you know me!' Shuffling over the pavement, the Albuquerque Tigers now zipped up against the rain, came the figure he had seen in the coffee shop a few hours earlier.

'Steve – you know – down at St Botolph's with your brother Ed and the others. Only I don't seem able to find them right now.' He looked at Barty more closely. 'Say, is there anything wrong?' His face became creased with worry as he considered the problem. Embarrassed, mortified, Barty tried to edge away. But Steve clamped a large, detaining hand on his shoulder.

'No, don't go. Let's talk it out, I'll surely be able to

help you.' Inspiration came to him, and his face shone. 'I know, have a hamburger.'

He led the way to a small white van drawn up a hundred yards away. Here an angry little foreigner sold hot dogs and Coca Cola to the hordes who poured out of the cinemas and theatres during the evening. He was always in trouble with the police for parking there, and with other hot dog vans who resented the commanding position he occupied, but in between appearances in the magistrates' court and fights with his rivals he managed to keep his end up.

Steve bought two hot dogs and looked around for a place to sit. It was too wet for the bench by the bus shelter so they finished up on the steps under the archway which led to one of the university buildings. Steve handed both hamburgers to Barty.

'You eat mine. I keep to non-animal food myself – find that meat muddies the thought-centres. Now what's it all about?'

Barty, his jaws glued up with doughy bread, could only shrug his shoulders.

'Is it school?' pursued Steve, his face again furrowed with concern. 'Some trouble about personal relationships perhaps?' This seemed to suggest some other topic, and his mind leapt in that direction. 'Now for a real dominant personality there's that sister of yours, she's a remarkable kid.'

Barty swallowed the ball of dough at a gulp. 'Huck?' he said, and instinctively he shrank away along the step.

Steve was instantly alerted. He leant forward, his adam's apple working with emotion. 'Tell me, does she dominate you?' He scrutinized Barty with deep earnestness.

All Barty's pent-up worry now burst out. It was not

that he felt any faith in Steve's ability to help him; in fact he found his interest embarrassing rather than otherwise. But he could no longer contain his fears; Huck had become frightening, and there was no one else to tell.

'I don't know what's happened to her. She's always made up stories, but we've never believed half of them – no one ever does, nor does she really. But now she does, and she sort of produces proofs – photographs and pictures and things – of people she says she's turned Jake and Polly into. She says it's because of a Time Machine. She says she goes off in it and sees these things that happened to our family, and she took Jake and Polly and she says she's changed them into our ancestors. Now she wants to try with Edward. Or me. I think she's gone mad, or turned into a witch or something.' Painfully Barty groped for the words – they poured so easily out of his brothers and sisters – that would express his feelings about what had happened.

But Steve, it seemed, had managed to disentangle quite enough. He was on fire with his interest. 'That Time Machine – I might have guessed it when I heard her talking. Tell me, does she read a lot?'

'Oh, yes,' said Barty fervently. 'Everything that comes into the house. They get sick of her at the library, she's always there so much, taking all our tickets too.'

'What sort of books, do you know? Fantasy books, say? Travels in time?'

'I suppose so.' Barty was vague. Huck always seemed to be surrounded with the sort of book that was meaningless to him, books full of long descriptions or of conversation. Sometimes she read bits aloud to him but though he supposed he could understand the individual words, strung together they conveyed nothing.

But his answer was enough for Steve. 'Fantasy!' he

said in an ecstasy. 'I'm your man. See this?' He tapped the badge pinned on his jacket. ' "Frodo lives!" Know what that's about?' Barty could only shake his head. 'J. R. R. Tolkien – *The Lord of the Rings* – greatest of them all. Oh, yes, if it's fantasy you're after I could tell you a bit, you ask those guys down at St Botolph's. And travels in time and children's books, I take them all in. An expert, you could call me. That sister of yours, she's been reading about travels in time. Now, my guess is that your house is full of old stuff about your family, so what's more natural than your sister gets a thing about your ancestors (lots of children's books about it these days, I'm currently making a study of just that) and starts thinking she could turn her own brothers and sisters into them. Oh boy, just wait till I get all this down on paper!' He had leapt to his feet and was jumping up and down beating one hand against the other.

Barty looked at him numbly. He could see Steve was excited, and that it was about Huck, but it was no help to him. The wet and the cold of the steps were creeping through his jeans, the hamburgers were finished; he stood up to go.

'Hey, wait a bit,' said Steve. 'We haven't dealt with your side of it yet.' He sat down and dragged Barty with him, fully prepared, it seemed, to spend the whole evening there. 'What effect is it all having on you? Here's this kid – Huck you call her? – with her dominant personality and her obsession about a Time Machine. Now if a kid like Huck is in some sort of relationship with another kid who hasn't got this strong personality, then the other kid can get drawn in under the spell. You follow me? The game becomes real to him too. Now, do you feel the game sort of overpowering you? Sort of becoming more real than you like?'

His eyes behind the moon-like glasses shone with

earnestness; Barty began to feel smothered by the weight of his interest. But there was no resisting Steve, even if Barty was not at all clear what he was talking about. 'They do seem different, Polly and Jake. But Jake's always fooling around, so it might be that, and Polly gets crazes for different things. But Huck says it's the Time Machine.'

'Yep, I can see all this is quite a problem for you.' Steve brooded. 'Now, what I think you ought to do is to hold on to reality. Treat yourself as the only real thing. Tell yourself that everybody else is a shadow. Ignore them when they get troublesome. Of course, it takes a bit of practice.'

'Ignore Huck?' said Barty incredulously. 'However much I practised I couldn't. She just . . . well, she goes on so.'

'You just have to learn ways of detaching yourself. Fix your mind on space.'

'How do I do that?' said Barty, aghast.

'We all have our different methods, of course. Some of them take years to perfect. Now for a beginner I'd say chanting something. "I am I and you are they" – I've known that help.'

Barty tried it out mentally. 'It doesn't seem to mean much,' he said doubtfully.

Steve made an airy gesture. 'It doesn't matter what it *means*, but if you say it enough and try to let everything else drift out of your mind – empty it, think of vacancy – then I reckon the troubles will disappear. It's hard at first, it gets easier. Any rate, you try it and let me know how you're doing. I'll be seeing you, I daresay; I want to call round at your place and get your sister talking.'

The streets were empty as Barty walked home. 'I am I and you are they,' he muttered as he turned the corner into Wellington Street. He screwed up his eyes and tried to think of nothing. But nothing suggested a round nought on the blackboard, and a blackboard wasn't nothing. Or an empty teacup, which reminded him of the chaos in the kitchen at home, which again brought him back to Polly. In the ferocity of concentration he shut his eyes tight, tripped over the kerb and fell flat.

It is always painful to fall heavily like that, and Barty was momentarily winded. Luckily the person who was standing on the pavement a few yards away did not notice him (even worse than the pain of falling is the embarrassment of being picked up and dusted down); nor did the woman who was shouting at her so angrily from her front door. Barty, skulking there in the shadows, trying to see whether the dark patch on his knee was mud or blood, could hear every word.

'I've had the lot, being asked how I was going to vote, and them as wanted me to be a Mormon, or buy encyclopedias or clothes pegs or give money to animals, and I reckon I can keep my temper as well as any – even when they come knocking at my door when I'm up to my eyes in pastry. But when it comes to people telling me I ought to keep my house clean – then I tell you I'm going to put the police on them!'

'I am sorry,' said the girl on the pavement stiffly, 'that you should take this attitude.' It was Polly's voice. Barty forgot about vacancy, he forgot about his wounded knee; he ran away as fast as he could.

# 10

'She's stinking awful, that's what she is,' said Huck bitterly. 'Do you know what she's making me do, on a Saturday morning too? I've got to go out and buy material with her, and then I've got to *sew* it, make it into aprons. Whoever wears aprons! I want to write poetry, I told her, but she won't listen. I don't know why people say that things were so much better in their young days. I can prove that they were worse; look what Polly's changed into, and Jake.'

'Look at Huck!' Jake came up behind her and tugged at her hair. 'And look at the face she makes, pretty little monster, ain't she? I'm off now, I've had enough of sisters.'

'Does *she* say you may?' demanded Huck. 'Stop pulling my hair. And let go of my arms, you pig-faced brute.' She struggled to wrench herself out of Jake's grip, kicking out at his shins at the same time.

'I keep hold of your arms till I'm clear of this house because I know what nasty little pinchers girls are. Do you know what we do with fellows' arms at school? We twist them behind their backs, like this. What, yelling already and I haven't begun!'

'Haven't you children anything better to do than to stand there brawling?' Polly was standing there; Polly in an unfamiliar mood, neatly combed, tightly buttoned into a coat instead of her poncho.

Huck stared at her with hostility. 'Yes I have. But you won't let me.'

'And I have too.' Jake thrust himself round the front

door. 'I'm going where no girls can dig me out, and catch me coming back before I need!'

'Who's going to get the lunch then?' demanded Huck. 'There wasn't any supper last night except that disgusting ravioli out of tins, and if anybody tries to make me eat it again for lunch I'll throw it in their face.'

'I'll go to Grants'.' Barty followed Jake hastily through the front door.

'*Not* Grants',' Huck yelled at him down the street. 'There's nothing decent there, we've tried it all.'

'I might get some ideas,' Barty shouted back. Then he ran as fast as he could take himself out of earshot.

It was not so much that he had expectations of Grants', as the faint hope that he might meet up with Mr Grant who might propose a joint shopping expedition. There was also the strong desire to keep out of the way of Polly in her strange new mood, and Huck who seemed in some extraordinary way to be able to bring about changes of mood in people.

But there was trouble in Wellington Street too. Barty knew it before he even pushed open the shop door. Through its glass he could see Mrs Grant on her legs. The bulk of her was enormous; he wondered how those doll-like legs in their high-heeled shoes didn't snap with the strain. And every inch of her purple flowered nylon overall was heaving and swelling with indignation; every lacquered yellow curl seemed to rise on her head as she harangued one of her customers.

' "I think you might be interested in one of my books," she said. "I doubt it," I said. "It has a message for you," she said, and do you know what she gives me – her no older than a student? There was two books (dirty old things they were too); one was about drink (*Mother's Ruin*, it was called – I'm not telling you any lies), and the other one was about gambling.'

'She *never*!'

Mrs Grant nodded her brassy curls. 'She did. Not that I read them, I pushed them back at her, of course. But you could tell as much as you wanted from the covers.'

'What did you say to her?'

'I gave her a piece of my mind, I can tell you that. "I've always been one for minding my own business," I said, "and I expect other folks to mind theirs – which they mostly do. But this goes beyond ordinary nosey-parkering," I said. "It's a libel, that's what it is, a court case – *Mother's Ruin* – me who never goes above my two port and lemon at the Lamb and Flag, and the pools and the Thursday bingo. If I was one of your vindictive sorts I'd go calling the police," I said. "I'm sorry you take it like that," she said. "Well I do," I said, "and there's many who'd take it a great deal worse," I said, "and no-body who'd take it any better." Mrs Gibbins down the way – she's got a nasty temper, mind – Mrs Gibbins had her telling her she ought to clean up her house, and she did ring the police.'

'Would it be one of the Jehovah's Witnesses, do you think?'

'Not this one. I know them, they smile and talk polite. She was a real hoity-toity miss, with a face sour as old vinegar. I haven't been insulted like that on my own door-step since the health visitor came round when Reg was a baby and said I was overweight and he was over-weight, and that overweight mothers made for over-weight babies. But I tell you who she reminded me of, that girl. You know them Huxtables? Like their eldest girl, only tidied up.' She sank back on her chair and closed her eyes. 'I just hope that Daddy remembers to bring the elevenses early today,' she said weakly. 'I feel proper used up. Reg, give him a shout.'

Reg did as he was told, then gave Barty a contemptuous look and turned his back. He made no secret of the fact that he thought shops would be all right if it were not for the customers. Barty, thankful for the lack of attention, crouched down and pretended to be deep in consideration of a shelf of rusted tins of Victoria plums. He hoped that Reg would allow him to look at these until Mr Grant arrived. Mr Grant came, solicitous, anxious.

'I got some doughnuts,' he said to Mrs Grant, 'one jam, one cream. I went out special. And there's your coffee. Is there anything else I could be fetching?' He hovered. Barty, intent on attracting Mr Grant's attention, straightened himself from the Victoria plums, and tiptoed over. Behind a stand stacked with pet food, he coughed nervously.

'If that's you, Ern,' said Mrs Grant fretfully, as she sipped at her coffee with closed eyes, 'you'd better get some throat pastilles. Or stop coughing. Nobody needs to cough, I read it in the paper last Sunday. It's just a bad habit.'

From behind her chair, Mr Grant shook his head and made gestures towards the door. Obeying them, Barty went outside and waited. A minute or so later Mr Grant came out, closing the door softly and cautiously. 'Well, that kitchen of yours cleaned up yet?'

Barty drooped. 'It isn't, not yet. My sister Polly says she's busy. But I just did wonder whether you'd be going shopping today and if I could come with you.'

'Not today I'm not,' said Mr Grant sharply. 'Catch me in all those crowds on a Saturday! What do you think I am? Besides, there's things to do upstairs – Mummy hasn't been her usual self this morning what with being put out last night by that girl. There's lots of you in your family, get one of them to go with you.'

Through the closed door Barty could see Mr Grant

lingering attentively by the chair in which the vast mountain of Mrs Grant reposed, then he wandered disconsolately off. He supposed that he had better try to find some pies in some shop in the town, but he slouched down towards the shopping centre without much feeling of purpose. As much as anything, he wanted to fill in time. Dreary grey wastes of it seemed to stretch ahead of him, lit by nothing that he could imagine himself wanting to do, and home as comfortless as the chilly, wind-swept streets outside.

'Cheer up,' said a female voice. 'It's not as bad as all that, is it?'

Coming out of his stupor, he found himself confronted by Polly's friends Susan and Caroline. They wore the same sort of clothes and looked much the same, to his eye anyway, but he had decided that Susan must be the one whose jeans were tucked into knee-high black boots. 'I was just thinking,' he said in some confusion, 'what I could get for lunch. I mean, meat, do you know how you buy it? I don't know how much to get, or what to ask for. Or how to cook it.'

There was a pause. 'I suppose I could *cook* it,' said Caroline at last. 'In fact I have cooked it, but I'm not much good with the raw product, I admit. What about you, Sue?'

'I wouldn't know where to start, not in a butcher's shop if that's what you mean.'

'I think I could learn to cook,' said Barty in despair. 'It's the buying. So I suppose we'll have to have pies.'

But the girls did not seem particularly interested in his problem. 'What we were looking for is Polly. Seen her? We went round to your place, but Edward said she wasn't there, and she's not at the prison though she said she was going to be. In fact, it's all rather a mystery because she was supposed to be on duty at nine o'clock and she isn't and the pickets are getting miffed. And that's an understatement.'

Barty remembered. 'She's gone shopping. With Huck.'

Caroline exploded. 'I call that pretty cool. The pickets were all her idea, she organized it and bullied us into it. Other people want to go shopping on Saturdays too.'

'Huck didn't,' said Barty.

'We've seen Huck though,' said Susan. 'Not with Polly, either. By herself; she seemed in a most peculiar state.'

A little shiver of apprehension went through Barty. 'She was furious at Polly making her go out shopping.'

'Oh, she wasn't furious, was she, Caro? Pleased with herself. She was just near your house, coming to look for you, I think. She had some extraordinary story about wanting to tell you about a nice Huxtable she had found. Somebody who would do for Edward, she said. Did you understand what she was going on about, Caro?'

'I wasn't listening. Barty, you look pretty gloombound, and I must say it seems hard they've left it all to you. If you like, we'll come along to help with the shopping and give moral support.'

'It's no good,' said Barty dolefully. 'I've just remembered. I've left the money at home. I was going to try for something at Grants', and then I decided not.'

'We'll come back with you, then. Polly may have got back by now and we can tell her what the pickets are saying about her.'

But Polly was not there. Nobody was. 'I say,' (Caroline had poked her head into the sitting-room) 'somebody's going to be busy. Look at this, Sue!'

Barty came and looked too. There were quantities of white material thrown down on the chairs. 'Huck said Polly wanted to do some sewing. This must be it.'

'Her latest ploy, I suppose,' said Caroline. 'Though I must say I'm surprised. I never thought sewing was one of her things.'

Barty wandered off to the kitchen. 'I can't find the purse,' he lamented. 'It's always kept on the dresser and it isn't there any more.' Then a thought suddenly occurred to him. 'Polly, she must have taken it. To pay for all that material, she couldn't possibly have enough money otherwise.'

'Typical of Polly.' The girls drifted in behind him. 'Never thinks of anything except her latest scheme.'

'If she thinks she's going to drag me behind her chariot wheels in this one, then she's very much mistaken,' said Susan. 'I can't sew and I'm not going to begin to try.'

'What are you going to do about the shopping, then?' Caroline was prowling round the kitchen, throwing open cupboards, peering at shelves. 'I don't mind helping you with a bit of cooking, if there's anything here to cook. Blimey, look at these rabbits! Who put those up on that shelf?'

'Dead!' said Susan accusingly. 'Poor things.'

Barty remembered them with horror. 'I put them there, to keep them out of the way of Thomas, he was sniffing around.'

'But is it your lunch or what?'

'Jake brought them home yesterday. I'd forgotten about them.'

'I saw my cousin skinning rabbits once,' said Caroline musingly. 'He made me watch. It fairly made me heave, but I wasn't going to let on to him, so I stayed, even when he started gutting them. Actually, it wasn't so bad in the end. I wonder if I could do it now – if you want to eat them for lunch, that is.'

'Not in front of me you don't,' said Susan retreating.

Barty stared unbelievingly at the dejected furry bodies. 'Do people eat rabbits, then?'

'Good lord, yes. Don't you Huxtables eat anything that isn't out of a frozen packet or a tin? I don't mind having a go. I quite like cooking as a matter of fact, only my mother never wants me around in the kitchen. Have you any recipe books, though? I mean, supposing I did get it skinned I'd have to know what to do with it then.' She stared at the chaos around her. 'No, it's pretty obvious you're not the sort of family that goes in for recipe books.'

'Is Mrs Beeton a recipe book?' said Barty doubtfully, remembering the huge volume that had belonged to a grandmother or a great-grandmother. To his eye, the pictures hardly showed food, they looked more like buildings. He had seen Huck poring hungrily over the coloured plates of jellies that seemed moulded out of stone, cakes apparently covered with plaster, puddings like castles. 'I can fetch that, if you like. It's in the book-room.'

'I'll come and help you find it,' said Susan enthusiastically.

Caroline was rather dubiously eyeing the rabbits that she held in either hand. 'Don't you go kidding me. You've had your eye on that room ever since you knew the house was clear of Polly. You want to go and scrounge around for bygones, I suppose, and brood over them and get squashy. All right, if Barty doesn't mind you hunting through the family treasures. But for heaven's sake stop twirling that key around – you'll brain someone. It's just the key of her house, Barty, not the prison key though you well might think it. She's staying with us because her parents are away.'

'My father has keys made large so they don't get lost. The trouble is they don't go in pockets then, not my sort

113

of pocket. OK, I'll put it on the dresser. But remind me, someone.'

Caroline was pushing the breakfast things to one end of the table. 'I want newspaper. And a knife. And bring that Mrs Beeton before you start grubbing around.'

But it was not Mrs Beeton that they came back with. 'Look at this, Caro. We found it lying on the desk on the bookroom. Who does it remind you of?'

Caroline put down her knife and peered at a flimsy, curling sepia photograph of a tall youth standing in a garden, his arm thrown protectively round the shoulders of a smaller boy.

'I suppose you mean it's like Edward, the little one like Barty.'

'That's what I said,' said Susan triumphantly. She turned the photograph over. ' "Ned and Bartle Huxtable, 1870",' she read out. 'Even the same names, isn't it odd? Barty says he's never seen it till now. He doesn't seem to like it at all, though. What have you got there, Barty?'

He was holding a gaudy postcard of the Statue of Liberty. He handed it over without a word.

'It's addressed to Huck. From your mother. Has it just come, then?' Caroline read out the few words that were scrawled on the back. ' "Just arrived. Lucky you caught me in time with passport. Hope baked beans didn't burn. Home next week. Love to all." '

'*Huck* gave it to her,' said Barty in amazement. 'It's what Huck said had happened.'

# 11

RULING lines and numbering them didn't help. Nor did, 'I am I and you are they.' Barty stared into space as Steve had recommended, but his mind was not empty at all, it was whirling. Mother had got the passport because Huck had given it to her. But until he had told Huck where it was she wouldn't have known where to find it, by which time Mother had been out of the house for a whole twenty-four hours.

He sat on in the bedroom behind the curtains that Jake – the old Jake, the real Jake – kept permanently closed. After a little he turned off the spotlights and huddled there in the gloom. Somebody came in through the front door – Polly? Yes, Polly; he heard her voice talking sharply in the kitchen and he heard somebody answering sharply back; then the sitting-room door below him closed with a snap.

Hours and hours later, it seemed, Caroline called him. She had smudges on her face and she was bristling with resentment. 'I don't know what's got into you all, I should have thought somebody could have given me a hand. It's not even my lunch I'm getting. I expect the rabbit will be uneatable anyway. I couldn't do any of the Beeton recipes because they wanted shoals of ingredients that of course you hadn't got, so I had to settle for boiling the brutes and even then I should have put in onions and carrots and things, and there weren't any.'

Susan emerged from the bookroom. 'Did you notice Polly's hair?' she said in an undertone to Caroline. 'It makes her look about ninety. She went past the door when I was sitting here. What were you talking about in the kitchen?'

'I really couldn't be bothered to listen. Some mad new scheme. Have you ever heard of something called the University Wives' and Daughters' Guild? No? Nor have I, but she seems to think we all ought to be beavering away at it. Not a word about me beavering away at those bloody rabbits.'

'And what about the prison? I mean, she made out the rota herself, she knows she ought to be there. Oh, hullo, Polly.'

The sitting-room door opened, and Polly stood there with a pair of cutting-out scissors held menacingly in one hand. Her presence was commanding, and the girls stepped back uneasily. 'Has Hannah come in?'

They didn't understand. 'Hannah? Do you mean one of the pickets? Was there somebody called that?'

Barty knew. He stared at her, appalled. 'I haven't seen her. She was going out with you, she said.'

'She ran away,' said Polly coldly. 'As soon as we left the house.'

'Oh, if you mean Huck,' said Susan, 'we saw her on our way here. She looked like a little witch, didn't she, Caro? She had an enormous cloak round her and she was padding along with a real oddity trailing behind her. I've seen him around before, you must know him. He's got an Albuquerque Tigers jacket, and shoes so big that he can't lift his feet from the ground. And a Donald Duck T-shirt. And brother, does he talk! Pubs and places pretty well bar their doors when they see him coming because all their customers leave if he goes in.'

There was an uneasy silence. Caroline changed the subject. 'There's that rabbit, if anybody wants it. I can't say I do, after what I've done to it. Anyway, Sue, you and I are on duty at the prison in a few minutes. Aren't you really going, Polly? They'll be pretty mad that you aren't there.'

'I have my district duties to attend to this afternoon,' said Polly haughtily.

There was another awkward pause. 'Do you mean something to do with that Guild you were talking about?' asked Caroline at last.

'You surely have heard of our work in the poorer districts of the town – our efforts to teach the inhabitants to live thriftily and wisely, to keep them out of the public houses, to give them suitable literature to read. And there is, of course, my sewing class for young servants. If Hannah comes in, you can tell her that one apron is cut out and ready to be tacked. I shall have to go now. If I call at this time I can be sure of finding both wives and husbands at home.'

'And blimey, will they be pleased to see you!' muttered Susan at Polly's departing back. 'Well, I don't know what's got into her this time, I'm sure.'

'She has her moods,' said Caroline philosophically. 'She could terrorize us all when she was as little as five. Even the teachers seemed to be frightened of her sometimes. Look, are we going to eat this animal or are we not?'

In the end, nobody did. Susan peered into the saucepan and said with a shudder that it reminded her too much of the corpses, and Barty had stomach for nothing. The girls, eating rolls and cheese, noticed how he had pushed away his plate.

'You do seem to be in a bad state today,' said Caroline at last. 'Is it because of everybody being out? Haven't you got anything to do? What about that Time Machine Huck goes on about – is that one of your inventions?'

'No!' said Barty.

But they were now intent on trying to bring themselves

down to his level and didn't notice his violence. 'We'll come and have a look at it, if you like,' said Caroline. 'Look, I'm going to give some of this rabbit to your cat as nobody seems interested.'

'The key isn't there,' said Barty desperately.

But it was. The Time Machine was squatting in its usual position by the bed. To Barty's eye it was no longer the interesting, problematic collection of finely-wrought rods and wires that he had brought back from the Meadow. Something – was it the crystal rod, was it Huck? – had invested it with a sinister, brooding power that unnerved him. The girls, however, seemed to notice nothing.

'What a thing!' said Caroline. 'It looks like some-body's efforts at modern sculpture. Though there's something a bit old-fashioned about it too – the way it's made.'

'I wonder what my mother would say if my little brother started putting this sort of stuff in her room,' said Susan. 'Oh well, as we're here we might as well have a go, I suppose.'

'Don't!' said Barty instinctively.

'I won't hurt it. Show us how it works.' Susan balanced herself on the saddle, her long, black-booted legs splayed out on either side. 'How do you make it start?'

'Try that crocodile,' suggested Caroline. 'But do hurry, Sue. If we don't get down to the prison they'll be so hungry they'll be eating the policemen.'

Susan pushed at the carved ivory. 'Nothing seems to be happening. I mean, shouldn't you hear it revving up or something? What am I doing wrong, Barty? Why are you screwing up your face like that? You look as if you're at the dentist.'

'He thinks you're going to break it, of course.'

Barty opened his eyes to see Susan heaving herself

up out of the saddle. Everything seemed unchanged. 'You don't feel giddy?' he blurted out. She stared at him in amazement.

'Why on earth should I? Oh, what's this clock thing? Should I have done something to that?'

'What does it say?' Barty darted forward and peered at it. 'Not 1870?'

'1870?'

But of course it wouldn't say 1870, Huck had had to come back; she was back. He was silent. Caroline looked at him uneasily.

'The family seems to have abandoned you. Would you like to come down to the prison with us? I expect they could do with more pickets. In fact, I don't know how much longer we can keep it going now that Polly's defected.'

Barty knew quite well that she didn't particularly want him, that she was trying to be kind. He went all the same; there was nothing else to do. It was as they were pushing their way through the jostling Saturday after-noon crowds in the Cornmarket that Susan pointed out the sight.

'That's what I mean about your sister being a witch. Just look at her.'

Huck had her black cloak pulled up round her ears and was sitting on the low wall of the church on the other side of the street. Beside her, looking rather like a dog begging for a biscuit, was Steve.

'Look at him – he's not talking, he's listening. He's even taking notes. Caro, I'm going to cross. I want to know what on earth she could be saying.'

'Well?' said Caroline when she came back.

'It was something about trains. I mean – *trains*? I wouldn't have thought either of them took the slightest interest. But she's describing funnels and things and he's writing it all down.'

'Oh, come on,' said Caroline impatiently. 'If he sees us he may start following us down to the prison, and he'd drive all the pickets away.'

But the situation at the prison had already sagged, if not wholly collapsed. There were now only some three or four girls. They sat on the steps, their shoulders hunched up round their ears to try to keep out the wind, their arms folded and pressed tight against them. The banners were tossed down in a careless heap. They looked up apathetically as Caroline and Susan approached.

'The others have gone, we couldn't keep them. You're late, you were supposed to be coming at one o'clock.'

'We were cooking lunch for the Huxtables,' said Caroline with a certain air of guilt.

'I don't know how you have the nerve to talk about lunch. All we've had is two peppermints that one of the police gave us. Polo Mints, those ones with holes in, not many calories in those. I was so hungry that I asked him if he could spare any more. (I mean, having to beg food off the fuzz, it lowers the tone of all this, doesn't it?) But he said we'd had the lot and he'd have to get himself some more, otherwise people would know when he'd been having half a pint on duty.'

'Polly wouldn't have let you take even one Polo,' said another girl. 'So you can count yourself lucky over that. Where *is* Polly anyway?' she demanded. 'She's the only one that can keep this lot together, and she hasn't showed up all morning.'

'She's *around*,' said Caroline, after a pause. 'But she seems to have taken up something else.'

'Something else! She was standing on these steps yesterday making us feel like worms because we weren't doing enough hours on duty and deserting the cause and letting the flames of revolution die down and I don't know what else. I felt as if I'd been lashed. What is this something else?'

'I don't know – preaching thrift and cleanliness to the masses. I wasn't really listening. She was teaching them how to sew, too.'

'Thrift and cleanliness and sewing? Polly? You're kidding!'

One of the policemen, his attention diverted by the flurry, came lounging over. 'Sounds as if you're talking about the one who's been stirring them all up in Wellington Street. Been knocking on their doors and lecturing them about keeping their houses clean and their kids off the street. Somebody rang us up about her, said she looked like a Huxtable. Like a Huxtable, I said, telling you to keep your kids off the street! Tell us another! When you think of the number of times we've had to rescue Huxtables from I don't know what – it's enough to make that old frump over there laugh herself silly.' He pointed to the statue of a plump and dogged Queen Victoria who stood, grimy and daubed with bird droppings, in the forecourt.

'I think I'm going,' said Barty. 'I've just seen someone.'

It was in fact Mr Grant. He was hovering uneasily a little distance away, trying, it would seem, to attract Barty's attention.

'They said down at your place that you were with those girls, and I knew from the evening papers that there had been girls carrying on down here. So I thought I'd have a try. And you are here.'

There was a long pause. Barty didn't know how to respond. Was Mr Grant after him because he had discovered that it was Polly who had so upset Mrs Grant the evening before? 'Who said I was with them?' he asked at last.

'Your sister, her with the curls and glasses, all wrapped up in a cloak. She was just coming down the street when I called. The lad who answered the door didn't seem to know where you were. Said he wanted to find you himself.'

'Wanted *me*?' Barty could not imagine either of his brothers ever bothering themselves about him. 'Who was it?'

'One of you lot, I suppose. The eldest of you, would it be? But different from usual, he had a collar and tie on.'

'Like a little witch', 'the eldest of you, but different from usual' . . . Barty stood frozen in the middle of the pavement, staring blankly. What was he going to find at home now?

'What I came to say was,' said Mr Grant, giving him a hasty look, 'was there anything I could be doing to help?'

'To help?' Barty repeated faintly.

'I mean – there you are with your mother away and you the only one with any sort of sense, it seems. I thought after you had gone from my shop this morning that it seemed a bit rough. I had my hands full then, what with Mummy not feeling herself, but this afternoon's a different matter. She's got her feet up in the lounge, and young Linda from over the way is helping Reg with the shop, so if there's anything I can do for you in the shopping line . . .?'

'I haven't got the housekeeping purse,' said Barty dully.

'No need to worry about that. I can put it down in the books back at the shop, and your mother can settle up.'

'What I say is,' said Mr Grant as they threaded their way through the Market, 'there's nothing like a kitchen and cooking for keeping a family together. The heart of the home, you might say. Gives them something to come back to. Mind you, it hasn't got to be the mum who's in it, I'm not one of your old-fashioned types who thinks that. I'm the one who's in it with us, and though I say it myself you couldn't have a happier family. Look at Mummy – she's someone to be really proud of.'

But Barty had seized on the word 'old-fashioned'. 'You don't think old-fashioned things are best then?' He asked it with an urgency that startled Mr Grant.

'What would you be meaning by "old-fashioned" then?'

'I mean, were people better, nicer, in the old days? Some people think so. If you could change people back – into what their ancestors were – supposing you could . . .?' He fumbled lamely for words, and then gave up hopelessly in mid-sentence.

'That I wouldn't,' said Mr Grant emphatically. 'Look at my dad, boozed away all his earnings, so's my mum had to go out charring most of her life. And bring up nine of us. Mind you, it probably was the making of us children, turned us out steady and hard-working like – we had to be or we'd have starved. It just goes to show there's a reason for everything that happens to us, though we may not know it at the time. But as for saying it was better in the past, or will be in the future – that's all gammon and it makes me really wild. Human nature's human nature, it doesn't change, and we've just got to learn to make the best of the people we live with. But what you people need is a kitchen. Do you know what I've been thinking,' said Mr Grant slowly. 'Would your mother like a DIY job done on her kitchen? Do it Yourself, you know. But done by me. I wouldn't charge her anything, only the cost of the materials. We could turn it into a kitchen like mine quite easy. And then maybe

I could come in and do a bit of the cordong blue stuff and show you how to do it, perhaps. You did say you liked that duck, didn't you?' he asked anxiously.

'Oh, yes,' said Barty eagerly. 'It was the best food any of us ever had.'

'My first try, but I thought it was a good one. And there's so much that I could be doing, I've been reading through some of my books and it's fairly got into my blood again. But Mummy and Reg, they like their cooking good and plain and it's no good thinking of anything else. Even that duck we did – and you know we had the fan on and the window open – well, Mummy still smelt the garlic when she came up and she made quite a poor meal that day. But if I could cook at your place – and you ate the stuff – then it would be a good turn to everybody.' Mr Grant hesitated, and looked doubtfully at Barty. 'I daresay I could fix things so I wouldn't be in anybody's way.'

'You wouldn't be in anybody's way,' Barty assured him. 'Nobody does any cooking in our house, and Mother hardly ever goes into the kitchen. Sometimes there are cleaning ladies who get food for us, but the last one left and there isn't anybody else. And I would really like to learn. But could our kitchen ever look like yours?' He thought of that miracle of stainless steel and glossy paint and shining floor in Wellington Street, and compared it with the dirt and confusion at home.

'Easy as easy – given a bit of time and elbow grease. I tell you what, then. We might just look in at Cooper's and price up things like cupboards and sink units. So's we can give your mother some idea.'

Barty had often scanned those shop windows, studying with longing their displays of streamlined kitchens and bathrooms. But it never occurred to him that anything from Cooper's could ever enter his own home.

He was running his hand down the gleaming steel of a draining board some ten minutes later, and imagining the difference it would make to the kitchen, when Mr Grant was suddenly transformed into a tiger.

'I've been watching you,' he roared, 'and I tell you I'll have no more of it! What do you think you are, anyway – a blooming bloodhound? No, I'm not going to put one of these units in my pocket, and yes, I've got the money to pay for six of them if I want. So clear off – see!'

Wheeling round to see the cause of the outburst, Barty saw Steve, blinking at them uneasily from behind a selection of chrome-plated taps.

'It was young Barty I was after,' he said. His adam's apple leapt up and down nervously.

'Do *you* know him?' Mr Grant took a step in front of Barty as he spoke, as though to protect him.

'It's someone my brother knows.' Barty was staring at him with horror.

'That's who it is, is it? Been padding round the place after us ever since we came in; thought he must be after shoplifters. Well, say what you want and clear off,' he told Steve. 'I can't abide being followed round.'

Steve shuffled round the taps to Barty. His Donald Duck shirt was competing with the Albuquerque Tigers; he had a bead necklace and a large Mickey Mouse watch so that he hardly looked like a store detective, unless Mr Grant thought they put on disguise.

'It was about your sister,' he said in an undertone. 'That was a wonderful story she was telling me.'

'Huck does tell good stories.' Barty was trying to convince himself as much as Steve.

'I'd like to tell it back to you and get your comments.' He pulled a large notebook from the zip-up portfolio that he was carrying under his arm. 'I took a great many notes – you need a scholarly approach to all this.'

Here Mr Grant came to the rescue. 'If you've finished your palavering, come here and cast your eye over this, Barty.'

It was a terrible half-hour. Steve had a story he was determined to impart – in fragments, maybe, but it was going to be told, and Barty's efforts to escape it were feeble in comparison. There was also Mr Grant to be reckoned with, and the tiger side of his nature was now uppermost. By a counterful of wastepipes Barty heard how Steve had met Huck coming out of the library, and that she had complained she had had to take refuge there from Polly who was making her life a misery, and Edward was fussing and worrying her.

'And I said I'd go along with her and she could tell me her problem and work it out on me and get it out of her system. (Sometimes psychologists make kids paint things out, or play-act their emotions, but I reckoned she was mature enough to talk.)'

'Barty,' shouted Mr Grant, '*when* you've finished, you might oblige by trying to remember how much space there is between your cooker and the wall.'

With his back pressed against a kitchen cabinet, while Mr Grant angrily examined the finish of various drawer handles, Barty got the first instalment. Huck had found a photograph of a great-great uncle and had set about turning Edward into him because she said she liked the photograph's face. Barty felt his legs growing weak under him.

'You see,' said Steve, eyes glinting, adam's apple working, 'the travelling in time theme. What we were discussing the other night. She brought the Time Machine into it too. She did this thing by Time Machine, she said. It's the details, she thinks of everything. She even gave your brother a pill to stop him getting travel sickness on his journey through time.'

'She's *given* it to him?' said Barty appalled. 'Already?' His eyes were on Mr Grant who, with a face that seemed to be swelling with rage, was pulling open cupboard doors and crashing them shut, but of this he noticed nothing.

'I mean,' said Steve near the revolving stand on which were mounted panels of kitchen wallpapers, 'she's got all her details right about the trains of the period.'

'What period?' Barty tried to pretend that he was passionately absorbed in wall-coverings.

'Didn't I tell you that? Your sister transported your brother Ed back to 1870, and found that he was a schoolboy on his way to one of your English public schools – Winchester, would that be right? And she went down to the railway station to see him off. That's where the trains come in. I mean, a kid could easily invent about a brother going off to school. But she could tell me all about what the station looked like, and the shape of the engine, and the colours of the carriages and what the station staff wore. I got it all down,' said Steve with modest pride, 'I always think these things should be approached from a scientific angle. And I read it out just now to a guy I happened to run into, a guy who I know is a railway specialist, and he was amazed, yes, really amazed. She'd got it all right, down to the last button. What do you think of that?'

'Huck does tell good stories.' Barty peered closely at a design featuring gaudy bunches of garlic and onions and tomatoes, 'if you've got time to listen.'

'But you see,' said Steve, his eyes huge behind the wire-framed glasses, 'I don't know that it is a story.'

'You told me that Huck played so hard that she believed everything she said. You said not to believe her but to think about something else.' Barty was now whirling the wallpaper panels round the stand so that they crashed against each other.

Mr Grant's angry hand pulled him away. 'If you don't look sharp you'll have the whole thing on top of you, to say nothing of the manager putting us both out into the street. I'd never have brought you here if I hadn't thought you were going to behave responsible-like. There's no call to be looking at any of them anyway. A chef doesn't want his mind took off his business by pictures of herbs and lobster pots and what have you. And you, whoever you may be,' he roared at Steve, 'stop pestering and wasting your time. You could buy yourself a pair of shoe-laces for a start.'

But Steve trailed them still. Barty could feel his presence, tense with emotion, somewhere in the background. Then, when Mr Grant was momentarily distracted, he managed to corner Barty for a last time, and pin him down among the bathroom display units. There, crouching beside an aubergine-coloured bidet with spray apparatus and taps gilt-plated, he made the final confidence.

'You see, you know I said your sister had a dominant personality? Well, she's succeeded in dominating me. She's gotten a hold on me, and I can't work it off.'

'You mean, you believe her?'

'I believe her,' said Steve dramatically.

'Can't you say that thing about I am I, that it's all shadows, like you told me?'

'They are not shadows,' intoned Steve, staring into space, 'they are the living truth!'

The wrathful figure of Mr Grant appeared round a shower cubicle. 'So this is where you've hidden yourself, is it? If you can't take no more interest than this then I'm off. No, it's no good saying you're sorry, you've said that umpteen times already and never acted sorry. It wasn't so bad while you still kept to kitchens, but now you've moved to *this* sort of outfit,' (Mr Grant swept an outraged look round the purple bathroom suite, its gold plumbing, its tiles festooned with writhing sea creatures) 'such as is only fit for someone's fancy girl, then I give up. But if you're in a better state on Monday and still want me, then you know where to find me.'

Outside Cooper's a tearing north-east wind tugged at the women's headscarves, blew dust into everybody's eyes and beat swirls of dirty paper round the ankles of the apathetic bus queues. Barty was running home. He might be in time to stop Huck, but it sounded as though it was too late. Panting down Simon Street, his breath coming in heaving gasps, he swerved into the gutter to dodge an approaching youth who seemed to have no intention of giving way. The youth was smiling benevolently down at him.

'My dear little fellow, you shouldn't have taken yourself off without telling me where you were going. Now, suppose I give you a hand with your Xenophon before we have tea?'

# 12

BARTY crouched in the porch of one of the abandoned houses in Hyde Street. It was certainly not a place where he would have chosen to spend a Sunday morning, but home was impossible now. He was not the only one who had been driven away. Huck had left a note announcing that she was spending the night with the Sopers; Jake had returned just to sleep and was off again as soon as it was light. Without them the place seemed desolate. They were certainly irritating enough when they were around, but in their absence he found himself lonelier than he had thought it possible to be. He could not talk to Polly and Edward in their extraordinary new mood. *They* talked to him certainly, to rebuke and exhort him, and Edward was urgent in pressing offers of help upon him. But Barty could only stare back at them dumbly, quite incapable of response. Steve's formula was useless in this situation because the new Edward would not give him a moment by himself.

Hyde Street was not an attractive place. It was a derelict street that the council had half-heartedly started to demolish, and had then suffered a change of mind. Most of the houses had their windows boarded up and their doors bricked in, but here and there was a porch which gave some shelter against the wind.

He stared out over the empty street. Such people as still lived there seemed mostly to be squatters, who kept to their own hours and slept, behind tattered apologies for curtains, for the first half of the day. Nothing stirred. Even the transistors which later on would blare out through the dirty window panes were silent. The wind blew a beer can up and down the gutter with a melancholy rattle. He concentrated on this. It was nearly nothing and would surely do for meditation. He screwed up his face and tried to think of the space inside it. The trouble was that its rattle so irritated him that he wanted to jump on it. So he crammed his hands over his ears to keep it out. But sounds broke through all the same, and now there were footsteps coming down the street. He leant forward to look.

'Huck!' he said incredulously.

She stopped, peered at him, and then hurried on. 'Is there any room there? I want to get out of the wind. If you push forward I can get in. I'll give you a share of this cloak if you like.'

Barty shifted himself to one side of the gritty step. 'I thought you were staying with the Sopers.'

'I was but they're going off to see their grandmother. Anyway, Lucy's so wet it isn't true. Soppy loopy Lucy,' she chanted from force of habit.

'Jake's gone off too.'

'Where's he?'

'I think he's got a sort of camp up the canal. He makes a fire and cooks things on it. But he says it's too cold to spend the night there. He said I could go with him if I wanted.'

'Why didn't you then?'

Barty shook his head. 'I don't know.' He stared at the tin, trying to imagine himself inside it now. It was hopeless. 'Huck,' he said, swivelling round to face her. 'What have you done?'

'Edward's turned into that boy Ned Huxtable. I left a picture of him in the bookroom, I thought you would have found it by now.' Compared to the usual Huck she seemed almost spiritless, like a balloon that was collapsing.

'I did see it, and the postcard from Mother. What I want to know is what's really happened. Not just one of your stories.'

Huck was getting angry. 'If you can't see now then you never will. Different people have got into Polly and Jake and Edward now. People who were once in our family – our ancestors. It's because of the Time Machine.'

'How could anything change because of that thing? – something I found on the rubbish tip!'

'I don't know how it could be. But it is. I thought it was one of my stories at first, when I was putting the bits of machine together. Even when I sat on the saddle I was still sort of pretending. And then it happened.'

'What happened?'

'What I told you. It seemed to rush into a tunnel, and there I was in the day before and Mother just going off in the taxi for the airport.'

'Steve says it's because you read too many books about travelling in time. He says the stories have taken you over.'

'That man's a nit,' said Huck furiously. 'He's wetter than Lucy Soper. He reads *children's* books, he said so; I grew out of that sort of thing years ago. You listen to me, not to him.'

'But the Time Machine doesn't work,' protested Barty, almost hopelessly now. 'Those girls, Polly's friends, tried and nothing happened. I saw them.'

'I don't suppose it would for them. It has to be somebody in the family.'

'Could they be pretending, do you think?' persisted Barty. 'Polly and Edward and Jake, I mean.'

'You know they never do things like pretend. Jake could, but not the others. I don't like it either,' Huck exploded. 'It was all right to begin with. Well, a bit frightening, but interesting. That time I went back to 1830 –

with Jake – it seemed as though it could almost have been a dream; even him talking like *Tom Brown's Schooldays* wasn't so extraordinary at first. It was when he wouldn't stop and I saw him with his catapult and peashooter that I guessed what had happened.'

'Why did you go on with Polly then?'

'Because I was so angry. So were you,' said Huck accusingly. 'I didn't know she'd turn out like she has – frightful old cow. (Do you know, she was trying to push me around to buy things for some sewing lessons yesterday! Out of the money for our *food*! I soon ran away from that.) And partly it was because I wanted to see whether the Time Machine was going to work again.'

'And now you've changed Edward,' lamented Barty.

'He looked so nice in the photograph. I thought it would be a change to have a brother around who did things for us instead of reading all the time.'

'You've got one now, then. He's making me do Greek – trying to.'

'Is that what he's making you do? He was telling me that I ought to obey Polly. That's why I went off to the Sopers.'

His chin hunched in his hands, Barty tried to work it out. 'When did it happen?' he said at last. 'About Edward?' He still could not bring himself to speak of the Time Machine.

'You went off yesterday, you said you were going to Grants'. Polly said I'd got to go with her, and I did – to the end of Simon Street. Then I ran home and pulled out one of the photograph albums from under the sofa in the bookroom. That picture fell out at once. I knew it was an omen, and I knew I had to do it. The Time Machine was sort of pulling me into it. Edward was in the bookroom and I said I wanted to show him something in Mother's room. So we got on the Time Machine, me holding the photograph. I made him take a travel pill and I didn't leave him very long,' said Huck defiantly. 'Only about five minutes of our time and then I went back to fetch him.'

'When you and the photograph and Edward went . . . back, what happened?'

'After we left the house (we must have been to see someone he knew; there was an old woman sitting in a chair in Mother's room. He called her "Nurse" and she kissed him goodbye), then we walked to Fyfield Road.'

'The same place that you found Polly in?'

'Yes, I think he must have been her brother. She wasn't there that I could see (probably bossing someone around somewhere else). You were, though.'

'Me?' Barty was horrified.

'Someone very like you. You were sitting in a room full of books, rather like our bookroom, but more books and much larger, and you were reading. Then when Edward came in you looked all guilty and sat on your book. Edward put his arm round your shoulder and asked about – Xenophon, that's what it sounded like. You looked guiltier still, and he made a little speech saying that he had promised Father that he would do his best to help you forward with your studies because Father had thought you had the makings of a good scholar in you, and surely you didn't wish him to break this sacred trust. Why, what's the matter?'

'That's just what Edward was saying to me yesterday. Just those words.'

'They sound like a book now, but they didn't then.'

'But *Father*!' repeated Barty. 'I can hardly remember him. And Greek, that was what Edward was wanting to teach me yesterday, he wouldn't leave me alone. I said I didn't know any Greek, but he said I only had to persevere with my verbs and I would find it getting easier and easier.'

'He said that to you in the Fyfield Road too.'

'What else did he say?'

'I didn't wait to hear. What I was afraid of was Polly coming in again, so I ran back to Simon Street.'

'How did you find him again – to bring him back home?'

'It was peculiar. I got back to the year I put on the time clock (which was a bit after 1870 but you know you can't tell the year properly) and when I left Simon Street and the old woman who was still in her chair there, I found myself walking down to the station, with you. And the station had steam trains in it, throwing up sparks and smoke and making a frightful noise, and there was Edward getting out of a carriage. He seemed very pleased to see us (he kissed me and I didn't mind), and he shook hands with you and said he thought you'd grown and were the daffodils in the garden out yet, and had the tortoises stopped hibernating, and how he was going to give you cricket practice in the parks these holidays.'

'Cricket practice – yes, he was talking about that too. It's horrible! You've *got* to stop it now.'

'You tell me how I can, then.'

Barty pulled himself away from the bit of Huck's cloak that he had wound round his shoulder. 'Do you mean you're going to leave them like that?'

'What can I do?' said Huck sulkily.

'You could take them back where they came from.'

'What's the good of that? Unless you want me to leave them there for ever. I've got to bring somebody back, haven't I, and I'd just be bringing the same people.'

'You never should have done it,' said Barty passionately. 'Playing around like that.'

135

'I told you, I never thought it would work.'

'But it did, and you went on.'

'Well, wouldn't you be curious if you'd invented a machine that really worked (only of course yours never do)? You'd want to try it out and see what happened. I didn't know it was going to make them so dreadful.'

'And now you mean they're stuck with other people inside them? But what's going to happen to them?'

'We'll just have to get used to them, I suppose. Anyway, Mother will soon be home and she'll stop Polly pushing me around.'

This started Barty on a new train of alarming speculations. 'What are people going to say about them? School and places? What are we going to tell Mother? And there's Jumbo tomorrow – police are trained to notice things.'

'Nobody seems to think they're very strange. Not Caroline and Susan anyway. They'll get used to them.'

'They haven't seen Edward yet. I mean – playing cricket! Everybody knows he only watches it.'

'People don't notice as much as you think.' Huck's mind was moving to something else. 'The thing is, I'm getting hungry. But I'm not going back to that house while Polly's in it.'

'You just said we've got to get used to her.'

'I'm not going to get used to her today, then. What's that bag you've got there?'

Barty passed it over. 'Just sliced loaf, and an orange. I grabbed them on the way out.'

Huck put her hand in. 'It's stale. Hot food is what I want. I bet Lucy Soper is having good food at her grandmother's. Anyway, I'm not going to sit here any more, it's too cold.'

They walked up the street. The residents were beginning to emerge now. Bedraggled, still tousled from the long Sunday morning lie-in, and clutching plastic carrier bags, they drifted up towards Meadow Street where a knot of shops catered for the needs of a clientele who kept erratic hours and who only thought of providing for the next meal when hunger pangs hit them.

'We could buy something at the Polish shop,' said Huck, 'they have lovely sausages.'

'I haven't got any money. The purse is at home.'

'Can't you go and get it? If I go Polly will catch me. She was talking yesterday of making me teach a Sunday school class.'

'You?'

'She said I was a privileged child and nobody was too young. I don't see why I'm a privileged child, everybody will be having much better dinners than us, I can smell them.' Huck came to a halt outside a Pakistani restaurant where the fumes of fried garlic were being pumped into the cold dingy street. 'Look, there's Steve. He bought me crisps yesterday; he might lend us some money.'

Before Barty could pull her back, Huck had rushed off to the shuffling figure who was making his way down Meadow Street in the plimsolls which he had still not found a satisfactory way of tying. Barty could see her gesticulating and explaining.

But Steve seemed to be in a trance-like state. 'Association with you is dangerous for me. I called up my psychiatrist last night and he said that clearly I had some sort of fixation and I'd much better keep away. It's that Time Machine – it's got me, like that.' Dramatically, he clapped his hand on Donald Duck.

'But you haven't got to go near the Time Machine,' said Huck, exasperated. 'You've only got to lend us some money. We'll pay you back tomorrow. You said you were going to buy some food there – just get enough for two more.'

Shaking his head dolefully, Steve disappeared into the restaurant. It was no use trying to see what he was up to inside; a dingy net curtain smothered the door, and the window was full of evergreen plants in plastic pots. Huck had to content herself with scrutinizing the menu again.

'I hope he won't get Madras chicken. I know that. You have to hang your tongue out between every mouthful to get it cool. We should have gone in with him.'

'He won't get anything with chicken in it. He says meat interferes with his thought-centres.'

'He's not one of them, is he? Those people who eat nuts and yoghurt sitting cross-legged on the floor? Lucy Soper's got a brother like that. I want meat. I'm going in to stop him.' Huck made a dash for the door.

Barty might have tried to pull her back, but he was staring down the street. 'Isn't that Polly and Edward in the distance?'

Huck wheeled round. 'They'll see us unless he hurries. If only he'd be quick we could get home first and lock ourselves in.'

Steve was behind them, three plastic tubs in his hand and a radiant smile on his face. 'I was looking at them ladling out the rice and I knew. I have to come to terms with that Time Machine, get to know it like you know it. From now onwards I live for the Time Machine alone!'

# 13

BARTY had gone to the front door for the milk. The milk wasn't there, it was still too early, but Steve was, sitting on the old pram chassis in the chill April dawn. He had spent most of Sunday afternoon and evening there; presumably he had spent the night too. When Barty put his head out Steve rose to his feet with a radiant smile, threw out his chest and pointed to the badge he was wearing. 'Frodo Lives!' had been replaced with a round bit of card inscribed 'The Time Machine Flies!'

Barty retreated to the kitchen, and because furious activity seemed the only way of knocking the frightful present situation out of his mind, he began clearing it. He was ruthless; everything was hurled out into the garden. He started with the old newspapers, boots, roller skates, shopping bags, that people had for years dropped, kicked or tossed into the nearest empty space. Then he followed up with the jars and tins encrusted with jams and pickles with which the family had grown bored before they were finished : these were thrown savagely into the dustbin.

He was in the garden, on the wrong side of the table which he was trying to drag down the steps – with the vague idea that when the kitchen was completely empty he might try to scrub the floor – when he heard the thundering knock on the front door. The table would neither go back into the kitchen nor could he pull it over the door ledge. He tried to crawl under it, but somebody was already running down the stairs.

'It's a telegram,' announced Huck, coming into the

kitchen. 'Shall I open it? What are you doing under the table? I thought it might be that Steve and I was coming to bash him. He's still there, though – do you think he's going to sit on that pram for the rest of his life, like those Indian gurus?' She stared round at the emptied kitchen. 'What a mess! I couldn't sleep for the noise you were making, dragging furniture and throwing things around.'

Barty got to his feet. 'Open that telegram – it may be important.'

'No, let me!' Huck snatched it away. ' "Plane arrives 16.15 Tuesday get a taxi and all come and meet me Mother." How nice, I like a long taxi ride. And just to-morrow too.'

'Tomorrow!' Barty repeated in dull horror. 'What are we going to do, about *them* – and there's that awful man on the doorstep.'

'They'll have to come, I suppose,' said Huck moodily. 'She did say "all" – but we're not taking him, that's flat, he'll just have to go on sitting.'

'But she'll see at once they're different. She mightn't even know who they are – I mean, coming back to find people who aren't your own children! And with a mad person sitting on your front doorstep who won't go and just talks about Time Machines.'

'I should think what Mother is going to notice is the kitchen. There's not even a table to eat off now. What's got into you?'

'I couldn't sleep – for thinking about them. We've got to do something.'

'I don't know what, then. Do you think,' said Huck speculatively, 'that our Edward, Polly and Jake are in the people in the past, and Jake is playing his drums and Polly making speeches outside prisons?'

'Oh, shut up. Could we ask Jumbo, do you think?'

'What on earth could he do?'

Barty indeed could hardly imagine. 'He makes useful suggestions sometimes,' he said lamely. 'Perhaps he knows of psychiatrists.'

'Psychiatrists!' said Huck scornfully. 'You'll be saying we ought to get Steve to help next.'

'Well, I am going to ask him, then,' said Barty with decision. 'He told us to come and see him today. I'll go early before the others.'

'And I bet you don't. You won't know how to start telling him.'

Huck of course was right. An hour later, as the two of them made their way to the police station, the nearer they got the more Barty's feet dragged.

'You're so slow,' complained Huck. 'They'll catch us up if you don't hurry. They've only got their coffee to drink.'

'I'm trying to think of the right way to put it. I can't think when I walk fast.'

'It's no good, he wouldn't believe you anyway. He'd probably think you were barmy, not them. And you might as well walk fast because you never were any good at saying anything.'

Sighing, Barty followed her. He would have to put all his hopes in Jumbo's goodwill.

But Jumbo was Superintendent Walker today. There was no trace of geniality in his expression; the craggy features looked rock-hard and forbidding. 'Yes, I know I told you to come down this morning, but I didn't mean you to dribble along in ones and twos in your own sweet time.'

'I just wanted . . .' Barty began lamely.

'You Huxtables want too much altogether, especially of the police's time. You'd better go and wait in the outside office until the others come.'

They stood in the bleak green and cream rectangle; you could hardly call it a room, or even an office, doors opened off it on every wall, there was not a chair to sit down on. The smell of Jeyes Fluid hung heavily in the air, far away, down concrete corridors, a solitary whistler could be heard. Huck padded round, peering short-sightedly at the sheaves of notices pinned to the walls – no Huxtable except Barty could resist print. But he was standing, by the door, watching the street, waiting for the strangers who were his brothers and sister. He could see them coming now. On an impulse he rushed over into a corner and crouched down with his fingers in his ears, facing the wall. 'I am I,' he kept saying.

It was a policeman who pulled him to his feet at last. 'What's got into you? You're wanted in there.' He jerked a thumb towards the superintendent's office. 'And I should step on it if I were you.'

Only Huck was there now, leaning against the desk. 'Was there something you wanted to say?' But the superintendent's voice clearly indicated that he did not expect Barty to say it. Barty shook his head. 'Then you'd better be off. I've given Polly the money – she seems to be in a more practical mood than you at the moment. Yes, I've heard all about you emptying the contents of the kitchen into the garden. That is not my idea of sens-ible housekeeping. My advice to you is to try to find something more constructive to do than that.'

'I knew you wouldn't,' said Huck triumphantly as they walked away from the police station. 'Where were you all the time anyway?'

'I stayed there, by the counter. I didn't want to see . . . them. What did Jumbo think of them?'

'He didn't seem to notice, really. But he was in an awful hurry, the telephone kept ringing and people were in and out. He just pushed money at Polly and went for

Jake. Did you know, he's been running round after the parties of tourists, and when they tip their heads back to look at a dreaming spire, zoink, he hits them from a peashooter.'

'I'm going to Father Fabian,' said Barty on an impulse.

'Whatever for?'

'He might be able to exorcize them, or something.'

'I bet you he wouldn't. And I bet you don't ask, either. Anyway, I'm not coming with you, I'm going home to try and get that money from Polly before she goes and spends it on something for her sewing classes. Oh, look, there's Caroline and Susan – over there, by Marks and Spencer's. I bet the people at the prison have given up now Polly's stopped pushing them around. Aren't you picketing?' she bellowed.

On the other side of the street the two girls looked at Huck with some distaste, then at each other, and finally crossed. 'The prison business has folded up,' said Caroline shortly. 'You couldn't expect it to keep going without Polly. She was round at our place yesterday as a matter of fact.'

'What doing?' Huck demanded eagerly. Desperately Barty grabbed at her elbow, hoping to stop whatever she might be on the point of pouring out now.

'She had Edward with her. She nearly drove my parents up the wall. They've never been too keen on her, anyway, they think she has a bad influence on me – all those sit-ins and things. But when Polly started lecturing Mummy on joining sewing guilds and seeing that the *au pair* girl went to Sunday classes (she kept on calling her a "young servant" too) Mummy pretty well went through the roof. She even told her that reading on a Sunday was setting a bad example to young servants. I ask you!'

'And Edward wouldn't leave your father alone all the time he was trying to get on with the gardening,' put in Susan.

'Yes, poor Daddy. He always reckons to potter on Sunday afternoons, and there was Edward whom he'd never in his life seen before, standing behind him giving advice, or just standing politely, which was even worse. We dropped all kinds of hints, but we couldn't get them to budge, and in the end Mummy and Daddy just had to get into the car and drive away. And Polly actually said she'd be back this morning with some improving reading – that's what she called it – for Marie-Claire.'

'We did wonder where they'd got to,' Huck announced.

Caroline looked at her suspiciously. 'They did say the door at your house was locked.'

'That's right, we locked it because of that Donald Duck man. He pesters us – doesn't he, Barty?' But Barty, with a hunted expression, was staring into the window of the nearby optician's.

'We met up with him yesterday,' said Susan. 'He was blethering about Time Machines.'

Huck gave a shriek. 'I bet the others forgot to lock the door to keep him out!' Scooping up her long skirts she was off. The girls watched her as she jostled her way through the Cornmarket shoppers.

'I should have thought the simplest thing was to let him carry the contraption away,' Susan remarked. 'I suppose you'll have to do something with it soon anyway, otherwise your mother will never be able to get into her bedroom when she comes home. Look, Caro, if there's going to be somebody in that house now we'd better go. We just want to collect the key I left on your dresser,' she explained to Barty. 'The key of our house, you must have noticed it, it was huge. It had a label with its address on.'

'It's still there,' Barty called back over his shoulder. He was making his way towards the Rectory before his resolution failed.

As he plodded down through the streets of neat little houses that had been built in the last century for the families from the iron works and the printing press that dominated this corner of the city, he told himself that this time he must speak out. He had failed when it came to Jumbo; with Father Fabian he must take a grip on himself. Surely that was what clergymen were for? – to cast evil spirits out of people, or at least to give advice about it. And there was only till tomorrow to do it; of course the Time Machine would have to leave Mother's bedroom when she came home, and heaven knows what would happen when that was moved.

St Wulfstan's Rectory stood by the huge Gothic church whose massive spire was the first to greet the visitor to this city of towers and spires as the train drew into the railway station from the south. The Rectory, a red brick barracks with bars on its ground-floor windows, was a forbidding place, long ago blackened by smoke from the railway yards near by, rearing itself up above the streets of tight little houses that clustered in its shadow, an eagle defending its young. Barty looked doubtfully at the shining brass on the door, at the newly whitened step, and then resolutely lifted his hand to the knocker.

The door was opened by the Rector's mother, a fierce, beady-eyed little old lady, who protected her son like a tigress, and a look from whom, it was said in the parish, could quell the most insistent tramp who called at the Rectory hoping for a free meal.

'Well?' she said aggressively.

It was a damping beginning, but peering past her into the shadows of the hall Barty could make out the figure of the Rector, in outdoor clothes.

'I just wanted to see Father Fabian for a moment,' he faltered.

Reluctantly old Mrs Fabian fell back an inch or two. 'Don't you go delaying the Rector then, he's on his way out.'

'That's quite all right, Mother,' said the Rector soothingly. 'Well, Barty (it is Barty, isn't it?), what can I do for you? Or was it your sister you wanted to see?'

Barty pulled back in horror. 'Polly? Is she here?'

'Not just yet, but I'm expecting her any minute.'

The Rector was looking enquiringly at Barty, waiting for him, obviously, to make the next move. But Barty, never very good at finding words to deal with unexpected situations, was for the moment completely thrown.

'It was just,' he said at last, 'that I was, well, worried about Polly. And Edward, and Jake too.'

'Those two big ones seemed well enough when they were here yesterday,' said Mrs Fabian sharply. 'A good deal too well, if you ask me.' She gave an indignant sniff.

'They were here yesterday?' repeated Barty.

'They came to lunch,' said Father Fabian, 'Polly and Edward, that is.'

'Invited themselves,' said his mother.

'They were full of zeal and goodwill then.' Father Fabian's manner suggested a certain amount of reproof, but his mother was not to be easily put down.

'That Polly, talking away, giving her opinions about this and that – the Easter flowers, how the Sunday school should be run. I don't know who she thinks she is, I'm sure.'

'We ought to be very glad of all offers to help,' said

Father Fabian mildly.

'She'll be driving all the other helpers away,' said his mother.

'No doubt she will learn to treat the – um – more senior ladies in the parish with less vehemence. All in good time. Meanwhile I am very glad she wants to make herself useful.'

'A thorough nuisance,' put in his mother.

'So I have suggested that she comes here this morning and helps sort out the books in my study.'

'Meaning that you're driven out of the house and I'll have to put the books to rights when she's gone.'

'And I suggested that Edward, who wants to help with the Boys' Club, should spend the morning putting a little distemper on the club premises. He offered to coach the lads in cricket. But not so many of them play cricket these days, and in any case our numbers are falling off somewhat. Still, the premises are still there and could do with some smartening up. Yes, a thoroughly good-hearted pair, your brother and sister.'

Barty did not catch Mrs Fabian's comment, but it sounded something like 'pesty young busybodies, if you asked her'.

Again Barty came away without a word having passed from his lips about his predicament.

# 14

THE door of the house was locked when Barty got back. His hammering and flapping of the letterbox brought feet down the hall, but it still did not open.

'Who's there?' Huck's voice called. 'Oh, it's only Barty,' he heard her shouting back. A key was turned and bolts pulled. 'We had to do this. Steve's been pestering. When I got back he was on the landing trying to get in to the Time Machine. But Caroline and Susan had locked up Mother's room. Come and look what we're doing.'

Voices echoed in the kitchen, as from a room stripped of all furnishing, feet rustled on newspaper, there was a smell of paint. Caroline was in there, and from the top of a stepladder Mr Grant peered down suspiciously.

'Oh, it's you,' he said, brightening. 'I thought it might be that Donald Duck. I can't be doing with him and that's a fact. I've known time-wasters and I've known nut-cases, but for a time-wasting nut-case he just about takes the biscuit. I can't see what he thinks he's up to, sitting out there. I know the wind has dropped and we might be in for a spell of spring weather at last, but if I wanted somewhere to sit at least I'd choose a door that had some paint on it and a step that was clean.'

'And personally I wouldn't choose a bit of old pram,' said Caroline. 'What's it doing there anyway? It can't have been yours; Mummy said that your mother never bothered about prams when you all were little, she just carted you round in a string bag or a rucksack.'

'Barty brought it home. He sometimes finds things on

the rubbish tip.' Huck dismissed the topic as a dull one, and addressed herself to Barty. 'We're going to paint the kitchen,' she said with the irritating air of one who had thought it all out for herself, 'and put in new cupboards and sinks and things, if Mother agrees, which she will. And I'm going to learn to cook, not ordinary stuff, but really grand cooking like that duck. I bet I'll be good at it. You can do the plain, I'll do the fancy. But first we've got to wash the old paint before we can put the new paint on, so get a cloth and help. Caroline's helping because Susan wants to look at things in our bookroom and I said she could.'

'I hope that's all right.' Caroline turned from the window frame that she was sandpapering. 'Polly and Edward don't seem to be around to ask. She wants to poke around again through your old albums and photos.'

Barty, however, was staring at the buckets of paint and the brushes, and up at Mr Grant. 'I thought . . .' he began.

'I know, I know. The fact is I got fair rattled on Saturday, but it was that Donald Duck's fault, I see it now. Then when I came round this morning first thing and saw what a grand job you'd done on clearing the kitchen, I thought I couldn't do better than make a start with helping you. I had some white emulsion by me so I reckoned I could do over the ceiling at any rate and we could get all the paintwork washed down ready to put on the undercoat . . . Now who's this?'

It was Susan, pushing her head round the kitchen door. 'Come and look what I've found!'

The album was too heavy to bring into the kitchen. It lay on top of the miscellaneous debris on the desk in the bookroom. On a brown page, covered with a film of thin paper which Susan impatiently flicked away, was mounted a large sepia photograph. Staring back at them, but separated by forgotten years, were twenty or more pairs of eyes. A group of women, some standing, some sitting very upright on chairs that seemed to have been brought down the steps from the dining-room behind, were assembled in a garden. From the oldest to the youngest they looked stern and purposeful; hair was tightly strained back from foreheads, bosoms strained at tightly fitting dresses. She pointed to the words printed below.

'The University Wives' and Daughters' Guild – the thing Polly was telling your mother about yesterday.'

'She'd have a job joining it though,' said Caroline. 'Look at the date – 1872.'

But Barty was looking for something else, scanning the names below it. It was there, Miss Mary Huxtable, and scanning the row of seated women he found her, Polly, determined, implacable, her hair tightly braided round her head. He looked sideways at Huck, wondering whether she would spot her too.

For the moment Huck's attention was on the names. 'Hersey,' she read out. 'I wonder if that's one of Horsey Hersey's ancestors. And look, Mary Huxtable! *That's* who Polly is, Mother's Great Aunt Mary. I remember all about her now, our grandmother told us. She did all sorts of good works when she was young. Then, when she was old she wanted votes for women. So she chained herself to railings, but nobody took much notice. So then she made a sort of a bomb (I don't think it was a very good one really), and she stood outside Oxford prison, but she threw it backwards by mistake and it landed in a horse-trough. Granny said her aim always was bad, she remembered playing croquet with her. Where's Polly in the photograph? There she is – she looks about eighteen or something. Aunt Mary was carrying on about votes before the Great War – when was that?'

'1914. Sue, I was going to tell you . . .'

'How old would that make Aunt Mary if she was eighteen in 1872?'

'For heaven's sake, Huck!' said Caroline with exasperation. 'Oh, about sixty I suppose. Sue, Mr Grant was saying there had been a bomb scare at the prison – lucky for all of us the picketing was finished, I bet our lot would have been the first the police thought of.'

'So Polly's going to turn into Great Aunt Mary – if we wait long enough. My sister is my great, great aunt,' Huck chanted raucously. 'She blew up the Houses of Parl-ee-marnt. Well, she might have if she thought about it.'

'I'm going back to the kitchen,' said Caroline. 'I can't take any more of this.'

But Barty was dragging Huck away. Preoccupied with her song, she hardly noticed until he pushed her into her bedroom and shut the door. The bed, which was a tangled muddle of blankets, sheets and the garments from which she daily chose the costume to suit her mood, stood in the middle of the room, marooned in a sea of books and comics. Barty kicked some of them away and turned round and shook Huck violently.

'Shut up!' he said between clenched teeth. 'Shut up, can't you?'

'Shut up yourself!' Huck tried to pull herself away. 'Why can't I sing what I like?'

'Because do you know what you're saying?'

'What am I saying then?'

'You're saying that Polly might be going to throw bombs.'

'Well, I suppose she might be.'

'Didn't you hear what Caroline said about a bomb scare at the prison?'

'I know she was talking about it.'

'Don't you see that Polly might have done it?'

Huck considered the matter. 'Great Aunt Mary didn't until she was about sixty.'

'We just don't know what she was like when she was young, or what she and Polly are like when they're mixed up. Polly was at the prison, she did try to bite policemen. What are we going to *do*? Even if she didn't do it this time she might do it any moment now. The police will be after her, I'm sure.'

Huck looked at him in surprise. 'I never thought you'd mind like this.'

'Not mind!' Barty almost shouted.

'You never seemed to care much about the family before. I've had an idea, though. We could lock Polly up. It would save her from the police. Just for a bit, until Mother gets home. It would stop her going on at us and organizing us too. In fact, it would be a good idea all round.'

Barty looked at her doubtfully. 'Lock her up here, do you mean?'

'Not here. That's the first place they'd look for her.' Huck's expression became very cunning. 'You know that key that was on the dresser?'

'Susan left it there.'

'Well, it had its address on it and I went and looked inside – yesterday. Don't look so shocked; I did and that's that. We could lock her up there, the house is quite empty, but if you're worried I could go and ask Susan how long it's going to be empty for.'

'I suppose we could find out whether she has been near the prison,' said Barty doubtfully. 'Just ask her.'

Huck was scornful. 'Ask her – I'll bet you don't dare! You didn't ask Jumbo, did you? Or Father Fabian? Well, then. Susan said there's going to be nobody in her house till after Easter. And I've got the key, nobody saw me take it.' She brandished the large iron object which had lain on the kitchen dresser for two days. 'Where is she, anyway?'

Barty remembered. 'She's down at the Rectory. At least, I think so.'


'You'll have to knock,' said Huck, when they got down to St Wulfstan's. 'Ma Fabian doesn't like me. She was very rude last jumble sale and said I couldn't try on that dress with the beads on it. I said did she want me to try it on in the road then and she said . . .'

But Barty had taken hold of the knocker which had fallen with a resounding crash. 'She'll be mad at that!' said Huck with relish.

The footsteps that came hurrying over the floor towards them sounded outraged, and the face that peered round at them was outraged indeed. 'What do you think you're doing making all that rumpus! There's a perfectly good bell, isn't there? Oh, it's you, you've been here once already. And the Rector's out now.'

'It was just about my sister. I mean, is she here?'

'She is, and she's doing a job of work, and I'm seeing she keeps at it.'

'Do you think we could see her for a moment?'

'If you youngsters think you can use this place as a rendezvous and a place to fool around in you can have another hard think. You've got your club-room and your club-nights and there's no need for you to come here at all. I won't have it, you understand, and that's final.'

'We've got to see her,' shouted Huck through the letter-box. 'I don't know who she thinks she is,' she grumbled to Barty, 'shutting people up like that. Well, at least it means Polly can't get at us.'

'But we've got to get at her. We can't let her wander round the place, throwing bombs – even if they do go backwards.'

'We could get over the garden wall,' said Huck after reflection. 'The study's on that side. Only you'll have to do the climbing. I can't in this skirt.'

She led the way down a side street to rusty iron gates which opened on to a small wharf. Here in the summer the holidaymakers who cruised the canal tied up their craft. It was empty now. A stained notice said 'Warning. Guard dogs on patrol', but the Huxtables knew better. The Rectory garden backed on to the wharf, and though they had never actually climbed over the wall they had sat on top of it and dared each other to defy Mrs Fabian.

It was only when Barty stood in the thicket of elder on the other side that he realized he had no plan in his head about his next move.

'Do hurry,' shouted Huck from the wharf. 'The wind's cold.'

Barty pushed his way forward through the dead snapping twigs, and emerged on a scrubby patch of lawn fringed on both sides with depressed laurel bushes. He bolted into these and in their shelter advanced on the house. A laurel bush was beating on the window on this side, and gingerly he straightened himself and peered in, cupping his hands round his eyes to penetrate the shadows. There were plenty of bookshelves, it might well be the study, and there was a figure at the far end who could be Polly. He rapped on the pane.

The figure started violently, turned round and strode to the window. Over the Rector's desk, with the glass between them, Barty and Polly confronted each other. Urgently he put his fingers to his lips and made gestures for her to open the window. Polly, grim-faced, impatiently wrenched at the catch and tried to raise the bottom pane – a difficult business since one cord was broken. At last she managed to haul it up a few inches. Crouched as she was over the desk with her head screwed sideways, it was difficult for her to be impressively angry.

'Just what do you think you're doing here?'

Barty didn't know. Gripping the sooty windowsill he stared blankly at Polly's furious face. Ideas, words, were racing round his mind, but too fast for him to snatch at them. After a long pause he said lamely, 'You've got to come, it's urgent.'

It was, he knew as he said it, completely inadequate, but to his astonishment Polly obeyed. She pulled the desk away, edged round it and heaved at the window. 'You'll have to push your end,' she said shortly.

Between them they managed to get it up a couple of feet, Polly scrambled out and they ran across the grass to the shelter of the elders. At least, Barty ran, certain that the gimlet eyes of Mrs Fabian were alert, and that any moment there would be a rapping on a window pane behind him, and a shrill summons for them to return.

'I thought you'd be coming out of the front door,' said Huck to Polly as she hauled herself to the top of the wall. 'Why ever didn't you?' she persisted.

Polly, however, seemed particularly eager to leave the Rectory behind and was striding out at a furious pace so that Huck had to trot to keep up. 'Did Ma Fabian lock you in, then?' Polly's lips pressed together angrily. Huck fell back and she poked Barty with her elbow. 'Old Ma Fabian went and locked Polly up,' she said loudly. Then suddenly she stopped in her tracks. 'Go away, you horrible Gollum,' she shouted down the road.

They were coming out into Meadow Street, and there, about a hundred yards away, approaching at a steady shamble was the instantly recognizable figure of Steve. He had seen them, and was stepping out as fast as his flapping plimsolls would allow. Huck cupped her hands round her mouth. 'Gollum!' she roared, 'get off! He'll understand that,' she remarked to Barty with satisfaction, 'as he's hooked on *The Lord of the Rings*. Don't you know who Gollum is, then? He's an awful flabby fishy thing who trails along everywhere after the hobbits.'

Polly had turned round at this disturbance too. 'I will not be pestered by that man any more,' she snapped. 'Hurry up, you two.'

'That's just what we want to do.' Huck charged forward. 'But he's on his way to have a sit-in at our house, so we'd better go this way, and try to shake him off.'

There was no stopping her, she pushed her way on at a smart trot, weaving through side roads of tall Victorian houses. Once these had been family homes; now they were divided into makeshift flats, their front gardens flattened to make room for cars. More cars were spilt along the street, and dustbins thronged what space there was left in front of the porches. At last they reached a road where the houses were rather wider, where the steps held fewer milk bottles and the doors fewer bells.

'This is Susan's house. Whatever do you think you're doing?'

'I know it's Susan's house,' said Huck leaping up the steps. 'I've got the key.'

She fumbled with the string with which she had tied it round her waist and pushed it into the keyhole of the massive Victorian door. She trod over the circulars that littered the tiled floor inside, opened the glass-paned door beyond, seized a key from a hook beside it, and went up the stairs two at a time.

'Huck!' shouted Polly from the hall.

'You come up!' a voice called from a landing above.

It is difficult to scold someone you cannot even see, and for five flights Huck was always round the next bend. When they caught her up at last she was standing just inside the door of what seemed to be a self-contained flat. Breathlessly they dragged themselves up the last uncarpeted stair and found themselves standing in somebody's sitting-room, looking down on a tangle of bare apple trees and flapping washing in gardens far below.

'There's plenty of food in the fridge because I've looked,' shouted Huck, dodging towards the door. 'And an electric fire to keep warm by. Come on, Barty, quick!'

# 15

'Supposing she gets unconscious or ill?' said Barty as they turned into Simon Street. 'And how long are we going to leave her there?'

'We'll have to let her out tomorrow morning,' said Huck gloomily. 'Because of going to the airport.'

'She'll have to spend a whole night there, then!' The enormity of what they had done was now sweeping over Barty. 'And what will we say to her when we let her out? She'll be mad with rage.'

'There's a bed, she can sleep on that. And bacon and things in the fridge which she can cook. Then tomorrow we can call for her in the taxi and she can't do much to us there. After that, Mother can take over. She'll be able to stop her throwing bombs, I daresay. Anyway,' said Huck joyfully, 'she's out of our way now and there's no one to nag at me and tell me to sew aprons instead of painting the kitchen and writing poetry. We've come back,' she bellowed into the house as she pushed open the front door. 'We're going to do some painting now. Why ever are you crying?'

Susan had appeared at the bookroom door with a tear-bright face, mopping her eyes with her sleeve, licking the tears that were near enough to her lips. She took no notice of them but went into the kitchen.

'Caro,' they heard her croaking, 'have you got a hand-kerchief?'

There was a sound of newspapers rustling on the floor. 'Don't bring that book in here,' said Caroline's voice. 'He's doing the ceiling, you'll get paint dripped all over it.

What's wrong – oh, it's your bygones, I suppose.'

In the hall Susan held out a green album with silver clasps. 'I found it in a box under the sofa. Somebody's even put in a sprig of rosemary and a pressed rose petal.' Her voice became thick with tears again. 'Oh, I can't bear it.'

Caroline took the book from her. 'It's a sort of scrap-book.'

'About one boy. They've put in all his letters and photographs and school reports, and little poems he wrote – everything. And he was so clever, and everybody loved him so much. You should see the letters he wrote to his little brother from school – asking about the dog and the tortoises and promising him help with his lessons in the holidays. And at the end his mother has written a little history of his life. He died at school when he was eighteen. He came home for the Easter holidays and didn't seem very well, sort of tired and languid, and then he went back to school and became really ill. You can see the letters that the headmaster wrote to his mother about him, and the letters he wrote himself. They called it brain fever. He died there at school. There's even a long account of his funeral and how his school-friends carried the coffin. I'll show you what his mother wrote to the little brother : "Our dear Ned, our perfect knight, left us today, St George's Day." '

'Ned !' Barty pushed his way forward. 'Ned Huxtable ! Let me look ! Where are the pictures?'

'Oh, everywhere. (Lend me a tissue, Caro.) From him in lace and ribbons, to him holding a cricket bat. There's one right at the end of him wearing a gown, called "Pre-fect of Hall" or something like that.'

Barty had found it. 'It's Edward !' He stabbed a finger at the face of the grave youth who stood there, in a scholar's gown, his hand resting on some books, gazing at them with a tranquil face out of the past.

'That's right – it's the same boy as that other picture you had, Ned and Bartle Huxtable.'

'Him and me!' shouted Barty. 'Huck!' He rushed into the kitchen. 'Edward's going to die, I've got to find him.'

They looked at him, amazed, Mr Grant with his brush against the ceiling, paint dribbling on to the floor, Huck crouched, reading the newspapers that were strewn there. 'St George's day, that's April 23rd, that's only two weeks away. Where *is* Edward?'

Caroline knew. 'He called in on his way back from the police station and said he was going up the canal to find Jake. Said he felt responsible for him. I did reckon that it was odd, not his usual style (though Sunday wasn't his usual style either). But not enough to make me think he's dying.'

Barty paid no attention. 'What does the book say about brain fever?' he demanded.

'If you mean what are the symptoms,' said Susan (astonishment had now stopped her tears), 'he just felt very tired. Then he got these terrible headaches and a high temperature. What are you doing?'

Barty was shoving his way through the rubble of kitchen furniture that he himself had dragged out into the garden earlier that morning. 'Getting a bicycle, of course. I've got to find Edward.' He was struggling to disentangle one from the heap that sprawled against the wall. 'Where is Jake anyway? You know, Huck, you were talking to him at the police station.'

'He goes somewhere up the canal, that's all I know. He did say something today about having a rat-hunt at one of the farms. But you're crazy – why should Edward die?'

'Why do you fool around with the Time Machine – you tell me that!'

Barty had only the vaguest idea where he was going when he pedalled down Meadow Street. He just knew that Jake, according to Huck, had gone down the canal where there were some stunning rats, and Edward had gone in search of Jake. The canal wound all the way to Birmingham, and there were probably scores of farms down the hundred-odd miles of it, but the boys were on foot, and there was a limit to the amount of ground they could have covered. He shot down the steep path by the hump-back bridge at Aristotle Lane and started on the long journey.

At the best of times, in mid-summer, the canal tow-path was not an easy ride. Now it was soft with mud from the heavy rains of March and he was on Polly's bike which was too big for him and threatened every moment to tip him through the rushes and rough grass at the edge, into the canal. Besides, there were people fishing, morose youths huddled under vast green umbrellas, with a sprawl of equipment round them that spread all over the path, so that every few yards Barty had to stop to lift the bike over fishing baskets, decayed loaves of bread, picnic apparatus, and plastic buckets in which maggots writhed. They stared on bleakly into the brown waters of the canal, and nobody offered to help.

Hampered by all this, Barty made slow progress up to Wolvercote bridge. After that, the fishermen thinned, but the path became more crumbled, and in some places had fallen completely into the water, so that he had to edge his way, on foot, along a slippery bank under the hedge.

The first farm came a little way beyond this. It was hardly a farm; more a cottage whose owner kept two of everything – bantam chickens, geese, ducks, a pair of pigs in a neat sty – and one sheep that cropped the grass by the fence. Barty was not going to leave a stone unturned, so he leaned the bike against the fence and made his way to the front porch. The owner clearly took as much pride in his garden as in his smallholding, for it was planted with little windmills, and there was a miniature pond in which two plastic storks watched their reflection and were watched in turn by bearded gnomes. There was a sharp rapping on a window pane, and Barty jumped violently and looked up. The window was pushed open and a head poked out; it was tied up in a chiffon headscarf under which the shape of rollers was clearly visible.

'What are you doing here? I won't have you boys around; if I've told you once I've told you a hundred times.'

'I was looking for my brother,' faltered Barty.

'Well, you won't find him here.'

'But have you any rats? I mean, that was what he was looking for.'

There was an outraged screech. 'Rats! The idea! I don't know what you think you're up to but you get yourself out of this place this instant, and tell your brother, whoever he may be, that if he shows his face here he'll have my husband after him with his stick.'

Barty fled, seized the bike, and bumped and swayed his way down the next half-mile of canal, braving in his hurry the pair of nesting swans that rose up out of the water with a terrifying clatter of outstretched flapping wings and hissed at him hoarsely with gaping beaks in which their tongues flickered like snakes.

The next farm was a dirty, derelict collection of ramshackle sheds, covered with rusting corrugated iron. Some starved-looking ponies nibbled at tufts of grass in a field that was pocked with muddy hoof-prints; there were pigs rooting in a marshy field. Certainly it looked the sort of place where you might well find rats, but of Edward and Jake there was not a sign, nor was there anyone to ask. Barty wandered round the outbuildings; wherever the farmer lived, it was not there.

There was a sound of a tractor coming down the rutted track that led into the oozy mud of the farmyard. It was driven by a surly man with matted black hair. Barty ran to meet it. 'I'm looking for my brother,' he shrieked against the noise of the tractor's engine.

'Haven't seed nobody.' The man climbed down stiffly and started pushing at an iron railing that did service as a gate.

'Or there might be two of them, one of eighteen, and a tall one with curly hair.'

The man never for an instant looked at him. 'I never seed nobody.'

'One of them might have been looking for rats,' persisted Barty.

The man swung round so savagely that Barty leapt back in fright. 'When I tells you I seed nobody, I means nobody, so git orf before there's trouble.'

Again Barty found himself lurching down the canal path. It was lonely country now. The railway that had run beside it on its way north had struck out in its own direction; even the sound of the traffic being pumped along the motor roads out of the city had faded. The last lock was half a mile behind; there was not a building in sight. On one side high hedges shut him off from what life might lie beyond; on the other, over the muddy waters of the canal, huge fields curved up to meet the sky. The solitude was so vast that Barty felt glad at the sound of a distant tractor over the horizon.

'Oi,' said a voice suddenly, very close to his ear. The fright was so great that Barty, who was trying to lift the bike over a tricky part where the path had dissolved into the canal, missed his footing and plunged ankle deep into the soft ooze. The bike fell on top of him and he wrestled frantically to stop its weight pushing him backwards into the water. There was nobody in sight.

'I say – Barty – young 'un !'

With a desperate effort, Barty crammed the bike against the hedge. Then he peered into the thicket of hawthorn and brambles. There was a figure just discernible on the far side. 'Jake !' he said disbelievingly.

'That's right.'

'How did you get there?'

'Through fields, a long way back. I daresay you could find a bit where the hedge is thinner, though. Wait a bit, I'll have a scout around.'

'I don't want . . . Jake, come back, I don't want to get over.'

But Jake was now a long way off. His voice came back thinly. 'It's not so bad here. I daresay I could give you a leg over.'

Barty gave the bike a last despairing kick to try to stop it rising out of the hedge and toppling into the water. Then he ran on in the direction of the voice. A long arm reached over the hawthorn and seized the shoulder of his anorak. To the sound of much crashing of undergrowth, Barty was dragged painfully through. When he opened his eyes (screwed up to avoid being blinded by brambles), he found himself standing in a ploughed field beside Jake, who was muddy, dishevelled, with bits of straw and dead leaf sticking to him.

'I've been looking for you,' he said breathlessly.

'So's big brother Edward.'

'Edward! You've seen him, then? Where is he? Is he all right?'

'Seemed all right to me. But I didn't wait to look. That's when I took to the fields. I heard him calling from the path so I legged it. Then I shook him off.'

'He was calling you? Did his voice sound weak – as though he was ill and tired?'

Jake stared at him in amazement. 'I didn't give myself time to ask about his health. I was off like a hare, I can tell you, before I got a sermon.'

'Then I'll have to find him. If he's on this path somewhere perhaps I can catch up.' He started to thrash his way back into the hedge. 'You go home and tell them that so far he's not ill.'

Jake looked shifty. 'I'm not going home just yet.'

Barty, who was trying to part the spiky twigs of hawthorn that tore at his clothes, looked back over his shoulder. 'Why not?'

'I'm lying low for a bit. The fact is,' said Jake edging nearer and speaking in a low voice, 'I think they're after me.'

'Not you too?'

'Who else are they after then? Not old Ned, surely? It was that gunpowder. I threw a cracker outside the prison yesterday – you should have heard the bang! And there was smoke too, clouds of it. I ran off, of course, but I've seen coppers around today and they've been giving me looks I don't fancy, so what with one thing and another I'm keeping away. I thought I might find somebody who was going up the canal who'd take me on board for a bit.'

'It was you, then? We all thought it might be Polly. We've locked her up because we thought it was her.'

It was Jake's turn to be incredulous. 'Polly – what would she be doing with gunpowder? She's even frightened of a Christmas cracker. What have you done with her, then?'

'We put her into a flat – in St Margaret's Road.'

'I'll go back, then,' said Jake with decision. 'I can't let

old Poll stand the racket. Let me get through that hedge and I'll run as quick as I can. Stop a bit, you had a bike. I'll take that.' He was through the hedge now and running down the path on the other side. 'Sorry about the bike,' he called back faintly. 'But a fellow has to stand by his sister.'

Barty lost all sense of time and distance as he trotted on. The canal writhed its way through the countryside like a wounded snake, swinging from side to side so that the factory chimney that he could see on the distant horizon seemed now in one direction, now in another, and never any nearer. And always there were the muddy waters of the canal on his one hand and the high hedge on the other. Probably Edward was no longer on the path anyway, but was striding over the fields somewhere else. The canal at least kept distance measurable.

It all seemed so remote from human life that he was quite startled when he came round a bend to see a lock, and, sitting on the gate staring down into the water, a figure with its back to him. He ran up.

'I'm looking for my brother. Have you seen . . .?'

The figure swung round. 'Edward!' said Barty. Then he flung himself at him. 'Do you feel ill? You mustn't die. I'll learn Greek, I'll do anything you like, but don't die!'

# 16

At the start of the journey home Barty felt exhilarated. Edward, after all, was found and kept assuring him that yes, he was in fine shape, never better, and certainly had not got a headache. But the exhilaration did not last long; after a mile or so Barty's feet began to drag. The canal was unchanging; brown water fringed by the gaunt brown skeletons of last summer's vegetation; the larks shrilled above the empty fields; occasional groups of lapwings flew up from the ploughland in black and white ribbons; otherwise there was nothing to break the monotony. Round every bend he hoped to see some landmark – one of the farms, perhaps, that would show him they were approaching territory that he knew – but the canal seemed determined never to bring them home.

'Do you think it's so very much farther?' he said faintly, leaning up against the wall of a bridge that carried a farm track over the canal into the deserted countryside.

Edward looked at his exhausted brother. 'You are quite played out, my poor little fellow. This is a long way for you to have come. At the very next farm we pass I will ask for a glass of milk for you.'

'Oh, no, don't do that.' Barty remembered with horror how he had been received at two farms already. Whatever might have been the custom in Ned Huxtable's day, he was sure that modern farmers did not expect to provide wayfarers with milk. 'I'll be all right.'

Somehow he limped, unseeing, over the miles that remained. Never had the little gardens of Meadow Street, running down to meet the canal, seemed more welcome. Then over the hump of the bridge at Aristotle Lane, down the rest of Meadow Street, and home. He staggered through the door on leaden legs and sank on the stairs.

'Is there any lunch for this little chap?' called Edward in a commanding voice. 'He's all in.'

People came out of the kitchen and stared. 'Lunch?' said Caroline, 'it's teatime! Heavens, yes, poor old Bart, he does look in a state, I'll try and find him something, though there's pretty fair chaos in the kitchen, I'm warning you. I mean, we're getting it straight, and Mr Grant promises us that it'll look lovely but at the moment we're at the stage when it's got to get worse before it gets better, if you see what I mean.'

Huck thrust herself forward and peered into Edward's face inquisitively. 'He doesn't look ill,' she announced. 'And look how far he's walked today. That Ned Huxtable couldn't have. I've been looking at that book too; his mother says in his last Easter holidays he didn't want to do anything but just tidy his books.'

Edward pulled at his nose, perplexed, and the familiar gesture mingling with the new personality revived all Barty's terror. 'What is this talk about my being ill? I have never to my knowledge felt fitter.'

'He thinks you're going to get brain fever,' said Huck, 'like that Ned Huxtable that Susan and I have been reading about.'

'I've discovered some more.' Susan's voice started quavering as she thought about it. 'Remember that pressed rose petal I showed you? He had his own plot in the garden, and there was a rose tree on it. His little brother used to look after it when Ned was away at school – his letters home ask about it. At the funeral the little brother sent primroses from his own garden – because of course it was too early for roses – and later on they picked a white rose to press in the album. "The last Rose of Summer" the mother called it.' Susan laid her head down on her knees; her shoulders heaved.

'She gets taken this way,' remarked Caroline. 'Victorian deaths are her speciality. It was really bad when we were doing *Dombey and Son* at school. It even got to the point that if you said "Paul Dombey" to her she started groping for a handkerchief. Oh, do dry them, Sue. I daresay if you'd met this boy you wouldn't have liked him at all.'

'She certainly wouldn't have liked Charles James Huxtable,' said Huck. 'Do you know what she found out about him? There was some frightful rebellion at school, the Great Barring-out, they called it. The boys locked themselves into the school buildings and bombarded the masters with desks and tiles they pulled off the floor. And Charles James managed to throw out a whole paving slab and he blinded somebody for life.'

'Huck,' said Barty savagely, 'you've got to come. Now.'

He had dragged her upstairs, pushed her into their mother's bedroom before Huck had had time to protest. 'Now,' he said with furious determination. 'You're going to do something. Only you can.'

'What can I do?' said Huck sulkily.

'You can try taking Edward back. You may find the other one there, or just taking him back may change him – I don't know. But at least you can try.'

Huck's face had become sullen and downcast. 'I can't,' she said finally. 'Because the Time Machine doesn't work any more.'

'Doesn't work! Is all you've been telling me make-up then?'

'It did work then. It doesn't now. No, I haven't tried

it, I can just tell. I mean, look at it.' She turned and aimed a kick at it. 'You could tell it worked before, it twinkled and sparkled. Now it's all gone dead. Surely even you can see that.'

It was difficult to tell whether it was the force of Huck's powers of suggestion, or whether Barty saw it for himself, but the Time Machine did now seem divested of the life that possessed it before. The crystal rod had dulled, it was just ordinary glass, and rather dirty and smudged at that.

'I suppose it's because I've stopped being interested.' Huck considered the matter with a detachment that infuriated Barty. 'And got interested in cooking instead.'

'Stopped being interested! When you've got all these wrong people locked up inside *them*! Well, you can bally well start getting interested again!' he exploded.

Huck was getting angry in her turn. 'You talk as if it's a thing you can switch on and off like a light. It's just gone out of me. It's as if . . .' she said, launching into her speech-making style . . . but she was interrupted by the sounds of pounding feet in the hall below, of angry exclamations, and a shout from Caroline.

'What bloody fool has gone and left the front door open!'

'Steve!' said Huck ferociously. But he had shuffled into the room before they had a chance.

'You see!' he said, pounding a clenched fist on his chest. Pinned on his jacket where once, bright orange, Frodo had lived, were two bits of cardboard. 'The Time Machine Flies!' they had seen before. It had now been joined by 'The Future Calls!' 'Green,' he said, pointing to them, 'to symbolize life.'

'If you mean the Time Machine flies into the future,' said Huck crossly, 'then it doesn't. Not this one. And it can't even go into the past now.'

'Nothing is impossible,' Steve asserted, 'to the true believer.'

'You can believe as much as you like, but this only went backwards. You can see the dial. Anyway there would have to be a second ivory handle. And I don't suppose there's another one in England like this; Mother brought it back from Africa.'

'Africa?' said Steve looking musingly at the Time Machine. Then he plodded out of the room. 'Africa!' they heard him repeat.

'Gollum would have made just those noises on the stairs,' said Huck with disgust, 'all squishy-squashy, slipslop – wet webbed feet, ugh. I never thought he'd go away as easily as that, though. Perhaps he's going to Africa.' She put her head out on the landing. 'Good riddance! Don't bother to come back!'

'Huck!' Barty pulled at her. 'It's beginning to twinkle, I'm sure it is.'

Huck turned to stare at it. 'It is a bit,' she conceded. 'I suppose it's because of that Steve. It's probably quite pleased at finding somebody who loves it like that.'

'Well then, why can't *you* try. Try with Edward. You don't want him to die, do you? He's downstairs, I'll go and fetch him.'

Edward was in the bookroom, lexicons spread open in front of him. He turned round from the desk. 'Restored now, Barty?' He smiled up at him. 'Then how about our Xenophon?'

'In a minute.' Barty hated himself for his falseness. 'But could you come upstairs first? We've got something we want to show you.'

He closed the bedroom door softly on them. Inside, Edward was stooping indulgently over the Time Machine while Huck, with sulky reluctance, explained the function of the different parts. Then he sat on the stairs, screwing up his face, clenching his fists. 'Make it work,' he kept saying. 'Take Ned away, bring back Edward.'

The house was very quiet now. He pulled away his fists from his ears. There was a rustle of papers in the sitting-room – Susan was there, brooding over the photograph albums – and from the kitchen the sound of water being squeezed out into a bucket as Caroline diligently went on with her self-appointed task of washing paint. That was all. He leaned forward, straining his ears, but behind the door a few feet away there was nothing but silence, not a voice, not a movement. It had worked then, they must have gone. He sat there for a few minutes longer, then scrambled to his feet and put his eye to the keyhole. He could only see floor. He rattled gently at the handle. 'Huck?' he called. 'Edward?' Then he flung the door open.

The room was deserted. Edward and Huck had vanished, so had the Time Machine. The rug where it had stood was rumpled, there were scraps of paper on the floor – relics of the dial Barty had cut out a few days before; the headscarf they had used to clean the crystal bar, the trail of earth that the Machine had left as Barty had carried it into the room. Otherwise it had gone as if it had never existed.

'Have you seen Edward and Huck?' he said, bursting into the sitting-room.

Susan raised a bemused face from the huge album she had spread on the floor. Obviously her mind was on the past, not the present. 'Edward was in the bookroom, that's why I came here.'

But of course he was not in the bookroom, hadn't Barty summoned him away himself?

'Seen them?' said Caroline, wringing out a cloth in the kitchen. 'I wish I had – I mean, not that they would be any particular use, but I do think that one or other of you Huxtables might give me a bit of help with this and not just leave it to Mr Grant and me. I quite enjoy domesticity, but there comes a point . . .'

'I'll come and help soon,' said Barty frantically.

He went into every room upstairs. You never knew, they might just have walked past him while he was sitting on the stairs with his eyes shut and ears blocked. There was nobody in any room. He came down from the top floor feeling limp and sick. How could he have been so crazy as to insist on this experiment! The wrong brother was better than none at all. At this very moment Huck and Edward might be wandering in the mazes of time, hopelessly lost, unable to come back, and nobody in the present able to reach them. At this thought, his legs became too weak to hold him, and he collapsed on the attic stairs. Then a sudden thought roused him. Could there have been a ladder outside the window? Might they have got out that way? He braced himself to go into the empty room again . . . and collided with a tall figure at the door.

'Look out,' called Huck from inside, 'Edward's going to throw up.'

It was certainly Edward, his hand over his mouth, striding to the bathroom.

'It's all because I couldn't find those travel pills,' said Huck furiously. 'I feel awful too. Don't boys make disgusting noises when they're being sick? I'm going downstairs.'

Barty followed her, almost sobbing in his relief. 'I never thought I'd see you again.'

'If you felt like that,' said Huck, flinging herself down on the sofa in the bookroom, 'why did you make us go?' Her face was pastry-coloured, and there were blue circles under her eyes. 'Anybody could tell by looking at the Time Machine that there wasn't any life in it – anyone

173

with any sense. And of course that's what happened, it ran out of life all the time. You can't think how awful that stopping and starting was, and the light whirling fast and then slow. Even talking about it makes me feel like I did on the Big Dipper at St Giles's Fair.' She closed her eyes. 'Get me a drink of water, can't you?'

When he came back Huck seemed already reviving. Her face had more colour and she was sitting up and fretfully trying to shift herself into a more comfortable position. 'I could write a history of Mother's bedroom — sometimes there were people sleeping in the room, they didn't see us of course. But we got stuck for ages with a woman who was undressing and she just shrieked and shrieked. I kept on telling her that I couldn't help it, I didn't want to see her horrible corsets, did I, and I'd go as soon as I could start the Machine. And once there was a little boy playing with a train on rails round the room, a train you had to wind up with a key. He didn't mind us at all, he told us he was saving up to buy a level crossing and a Fyffes banana van.'

'But Edward,' said Barty in agony. 'What was happening to him?'

'He was just trying to keep his balance and I was holding on to one of his legs.'

'I mean, did you get him back to 1870? Have you changed him?'

'I don't know whether he's changed or not because he rushed off to be sick as soon as we got back. But we didn't get back to 1870, nothing like. The dial hand kept sticking at 1900. Do you know what I think's happened?' said Huck slowly. 'I think it's what that Steve has been saying about the Future in front of it that's upset it. It's obviously very delicately made, like one of your old computers that you say can have nervous breakdowns if you feed the wrong information in. And now the Time Machine doesn't know whether it's made for the Past or the Future so it zigzags around. If I see him again,' she said grimly, grinding her teeth – then she heaved herself up on her elbow and peered at the window – 'Is that him who's just gone past?'

'It's Jake!' Barty ran into the hall to meet him. 'Jake! I found Edward!' Then he faltered and stopped, remembering that inside this familiar slouching figure was an unknown person, capable, apparently, of violence that went far beyond peashooters and catapults. 'Are you all right?' he said lamely. 'I mean, has there been any trouble at school – or anything?'

Jake was outraged. 'At school? What do you go jawing about school for in the holidays! You're as bad as Edward. Anyway, it's Poll who's in trouble now.'

'Polly!' Barty's mind leapt from Charles James Huxtable and the battle between masters and boys to Great Aunt Mary and her bomb.

'She's locked up, on a top floor in St Margaret's Road. I went up and down the place looking, after what you said down the canal. Only you didn't say what number, so blessed if I didn't have to knock on all the doors and ask for her. Then if I couldn't get an answer I went round their back gardens hollering. It's taken me all afternoon, but I've got her now – leastways, I would have if I could get her out. She says you've got the key, though.'

'Huck.' Barty went back into the bookroom. 'You've got the key. You know, of Susan's house.'

'What are you whispering for?' said Huck fretfully.

'The key you took. You had it tied round you. You don't want everyone to know you took it, do you? And Susan's in the sitting-room.'

'We don't want Polly,' said Huck decidedly. 'Not yet. She can wait till tomorrow morning.'

Barty lost his temper, and his voice rose. 'She can't

wait, we've got to let her out.'

'You put her in, didn't you? You said you were frightened of her throwing a bomb.'

'Well, she didn't. Jake said the bomb scare was because of him chucking a firework.'

'She still might, I suppose. Anyway, we can't let her out because the key's gone. It must have fallen off me while the old Machine was bucketing around in time, and we'll never find it now.' She stiffened. 'Look, it is that Steve now. He's got it coming to him, I can tell you.'

# 17

THE bell on the front door had long ago stopped working, otherwise Steve no doubt would have used that too. As it was he hammered with the knocker, flapped the letterbox, and made such noise with his feet as a pair of over-size canvas shoes allowed.

Huck ran into the hall in a fury. 'I'm going to make him stop it – banging and shouting like that! I should think I'd get brain fever after this.'

The flap of the letterbox had been pushed open; they could see the fingers that had done it, and there seemed to be a face too. Huck seized an umbrella and charged. Mercifully her aim was wild. The umbrella hit the door, broke, and she was left holding the handle. With only one idea – violence – she pulled savagely at the bolts, and before anybody realized what she was up to she was standing at the open door, the umbrella handle raised above her head like a club, and Steve sprawled over the threshold, prostrate at her feet, one hand still clutching a small crocodile carved out of what seemed to be an elephant's tusk.

'That's *my* crocodile!' Huck flung down the handle and tried to wrench the ivory from him.

'The Future!' crooned Steve, who was scrambling to all fours as best he could while trying to pull the tusk from Huck and to search blindly behind him with a naked foot for the plimsoll that had escaped on the pavement. At last he was upright and confronting them with a radiant face. He held the crocodile high above his head. 'The Sacred Flame! The Key to the Future!'

Huck jumped to try to reach it. 'I don't know how you got it, but you're going to give it back. Don't just stand there, make him!' she shouted over her shoulder. 'He's stolen it from the Time Machine!'

Steve cradled the crocodile protectively. 'This is no stolen goods. The Time Machine would reject it; it cannot be sullied with Impurity. Africa you told me, from Africa it has come!'

'So did mine come from Africa. Let me see it. I'd know mine anywhere, its tail is chipped.'

Steve displayed it. This crocodile was perfect, from its toothy, widely-gaping jaws to the last scale on its back. 'Where did it come from, then?' demanded Huck.

'From the Dark Continent!' Steve made it sound like some incantation.

'You mean the shop in Wellington Street?' They all knew the place, where an immensely tall, bearded African, his face ritually scarred, sat among a collection of savage-looking objects. It was certainly not a shop for the idly curious. Even Jake – the old Jake – had slunk away from that statuesque and watchful presence without so much as picking up one of the figurines or pots, or tapping a drum.

'Not a shop,' reproved Steve, 'a treasure house.'

'Are you going to try it?' said Huck. Clearly, her interest had been whetted. 'If you are I'm going to be there.'

'Without you, Time stands still!' announced Steve.

Stupefied, Barty watched them : Huck running on ahead up the stairs, Steve plodding as fast as his plimsolls would let him. Then he came to his senses and chased after them. They were standing by the Time Machine when Barty burst into his mother's room. Wherever it had been last time he had looked, it had returned and sat in its old place, on the rug. But he knew without looking at it that it had changed, and when they moved away he could see; it had its old wicked gleam, it was alive again, trembling to take off.

Huck turned. 'You'll have to help. It needs you. You've got to get this other crocodile in and make a new dial. Otherwise we can't go to the Future.'

'The Collaboration of the Two Minds!' Steve seemed to be in a frenzy of excitement. 'Fact, and Fancy.' He gestured first at Barty, then at Huck.

'I always wanted to go to the Future,' said Huck, almost as excited as Steve. 'Like the Time Traveller. I could take Edward and Polly and Jake there too. It may cure them.'

Barty took a step forward. 'No!' he said fiercely.

Huck was offended. 'I said that because I thought it would please you.'

'I mean, no, you're not going to the Future. You're not going anywhere any more.'

And Barty strode forward, scooped up the Machine, banged the door, locked it, and staggered downstairs. The noise that he made dragging it down was drowned by the shouts and ferocity of the battery of blows that were being rained on the door upstairs. Susan and Caroline appeared.

'What on earth is going on?'

'I've got to get this away from those two.' Barty was struggling to get it clear of the banisters.

'You'll have to be quick then if you want to do it before those two smash their way out.'

'Or before I smash my way in,' said a voice at the open front door. 'Good God Almighty, isn't there ever a moment when this house of yours is quiet! They warned us when we moved in that it wouldn't be any rest cure, living next door to the Huxtables, and I reckoned that after three weeks of you we knew everything there was to be known about noise. What I didn't know was that you were going to start demolishing the house today. Can you give me an axe, someone, so that I can join in?'

Barty paid no attention. He shoved his way past the angry, bearded figure in the doorway, hooked the pram chassis towards him with one foot, thrust the monstrous erection upon it, and started on his journey. Upstairs, it sounded as though a chair was being hurled at the door panels.

As soon as the Machine was balanced on the wheels he knew where he had to take it – back to the rubbish tip where it belonged, where it could get buried again, and lose itself in the city's debris. Before, he had dragged it home at his leisure, making frequent stops to straighten his aching back. Now it was a race. Bent double over the wheels, able to see only through a network of wires, pushing with one hand, trying to hold the structure steady with the other, he felt it was an achievement even to get it to the end of Simon Street. Somehow he managed to turn the corner into Wellington Street without it falling off the pram, and there was a moment or two of panic as he crossed over Meadow Street with it, and tried to get the front wheels up over the high kerb on the other side with an oncoming bus only a few yards away.

The Press clock told him that it was nearly five; it would not be long now before the works people would be surging from the iron foundry farther up the road. Gasping, sweating, his hair flopping into his eyes, heedless of the passers-by whose shins he grazed, he pushed on. At Iron Street the escaping hordes met him. Wave upon wave of bicycles, motor bikes, cars, in the road – the narrow pavements packed with a solid mass of solid men determined to get home to their tea – he was brought to a standstill, and could only crouch there while the impatient throng pushed past. Desperately he looked back over his shoulder; the pursuers might almost be on his heels but he would never be able to see them.

When the mob in Iron Street thinned down to a straggling few, he started again. But there was a new danger. Before, the crowds had given him cover; now he could be seen the length of the street. He launched the wheels into the road – no kerbs to cope with there – and struggled to make up for lost time.

Down the slope outside the gates of the iron works (the wheels nearly ran away with him there), up the hill towards the bridge that crossed the railway and the canal, the blood hammering in his ears and a red mist in front of his eyes. But pushing the thing up was nothing to the effort needed to keep it under control when it was going down. It took charge on the other side of the bridge, and Barty's arms were nearly dragged out of their sockets. The five-bar gate that led on to the Meadow stopped its headlong journey, and with cramped, numbed fingers Barty fumbled to open this. Shutting it behind him he saw what he had been expecting and dreading all the time, Steve, just coming over the crest of the bridge. 'Hi!' a voice came thinly down the wind towards him. 'Hi! Stop there!'

There was still a quarter of a mile between Barty and the rubbish tip, and it was a question of whether he and his top-heavy burden could reach it before Steve, shuffling in the plimsolls that allowed for no running. He was tiring now, and the wheels shot this way and that, rambling all over the concrete track and making for extra effort while they took him no farther. The willow trees that marked the margin of the tip seemed as remote as ever; but Steve's voice (he dared not turn round and look) grew surely closer. 'Every step takes you nearer,' he remembered some grown-up saying to him when he was small. 'Put your feet in front of each other and you'll get there.' So now he concentrated on that: pushing; putting one foot in front; then another; just again; then again.

There was a jolt. The wheels came to a stop. Barty felt the whole structure tipping, swaying, and was just in time to clutch the frame of the Machine before it could follow the wheels into the ditch. He had reached the willows and the muddy creek that bounded the meadow land, but though the wheels might have given up Barty could not. He must lose this dangerous object in one of the pits and holes on the other side of the gate. There was no time now to try to open it; besides, it was probably padlocked. Making a last, tremendous effort, he lifted the Machine high enough to hurl it over. There was a howl from behind him, and when Barty jumped down on the other side he saw Steve some twenty yards away, his face contorted with dismay.

It was now a question of trying to outstrip Steve and of finding a hiding place, but as Barty dragged it up and down the hillocks of dead leaves and soft earth he realized how useless it was, and marvelled that he had ever started on this crazy journey. Of course the Time Machine was far too big to hide just like that. It had been buried when he found it, and there was not now the smallest chance that he could outdistance Steve for long enough either to dig it in or to find a place to conceal its bulk. But all the same he staggered on, too weary now to think of any alternative. Or to look where he was going. He had caught his foot in something, he felt himself falling, falling – a process that seemed to take whole minutes while he thought dully that this was the end of it all, that he might just as well have never set out.

He could not be bothered to look up. He lay there with his face pressed in the cold leaves. He heard the rustling as Steve plunged past him, the excited exclamations, and then a wail. His shoulder was shaken.

'Where is it? What've you done with it?'

Barty rolled over and sat up. 'It's there, isn't it?'

'The Life Force!' said Steve wildly. 'Gone!' He pulled Barty to his feet and dragged him over. 'Look there!'

The Machine lay tumbled on its side in a hollow. The cushion which Huck had stuffed over the saddle springs had long ago fallen off, but the crocodile tusk – Huck's – was still there. Barty pulled it out; yes, her crocodile with the tip of its tail snapped off. He pushed it in his pocket. The Time Machine lay there, but looking like a Time Machine no longer, just a curious medley of rods, rather dirty, that would soon be swallowed up and disappear into the anonymity of the rubbish dump.

'The crystal bar has gone,' said Barty, noticing suddenly.

'The Life Force! That's what I'm telling you. Where is it? What have you done with it?'

'I didn't do anything. It must have fallen off when I wasn't noticing. It could be anywhere.'

With a strangled cry Steve fell on his knees and started groping. 'I will sift this place inch by inch. I will not leave till I have found you, my Precious.'

Barty stared down at the close-cropped head, the rounded back, the pallid soles of the canvas shoes, of the figure that crawled over the earth. 'Inch by inch, my Precious,' he heard him whimpering.

Barty left him there.

# 18

BARTY could hear Jake's drum long before he reached the house. It seemed to be what he had been expecting; he didn't feel any surprise. When he pushed open the front door, Huck came out of the kitchen with a brush that dripped white paint. Barty snuffed the smell with pleasure.

'You've been a long time. What have you done with Steve? He went chasing after you when that bearded man from next door made Susan and Caroline let us out. They stopped me, though. I didn't care; I'm finishing off painting one of the walls. We've had an idea about supper. We're going to get a take-away meal from the Chinese place and make a fire down by the canal somewhere and eat it there – the kitchen won't be ready for days yet.'

'Who's we?'

Huck stared. 'Edward and Polly and Jake and you and me, of course. Who do you think? Mr Grant went home ages ago, and Caroline and Susan have gone. Oh, and I found the key of Susan's house, it was on the rug by Mother's bed – under where your old machine was – so Jake went off and let Polly out.'

'Was she very angry?'

Huck shrugged. 'Not particularly. She's in the sitting-room. I'm going back to the painting.'

Polly lifted her head from the material that she was crouching over and looked at Barty as he loitered by the sitting-room door. 'You were a dope, locking me in like that. Yes, I know Jake said it was because you had some mad idea that I'd throw a bomb, but you could have asked, couldn't you? Anyway, it's turned out quite well because on his way to let me out Jake met up with Jumbo and he said no taxi could get six of us in so he'll take the day off tomorrow and drive us all up to Heathrow to meet Mother. So if you've ordered a taxi, cancel it.'

'I hadn't. There seemed to be so many other things.' Barty lingered still. 'What are you sewing? Aprons?'

'Aprons?' said Polly in amazement. 'Whatever would I be doing with aprons? Our form's putting on a play next term, and I'm going to have a masque of the ghosts of oppressed women in it – these are for them, if I can get the others to stitch them. But Sue and Caro seem more interested in painting the kitchen at the moment. Some people take a lot of driving.'

The drums had stopped. The ceiling shook under Jake's feet on the floor above.

'That boy,' remarked Polly, picking up her scissors again, 'he'll get himself lynched one of these days. Some of the neighbours are getting quite violent.'

'There's gratitude for you,' said Jake's voice from the hall. 'When I do my best to provide stimulus and entertainment for the inhabitants of Simon Street. They don't deserve my genius, that's all I can say. Why, if it isn't our Ed, looking quite animated. What's the evening paper got in it, Ed, that brings such a flush to the pallid scholarly cheek and such ink to the nose?'

Barty turned. Edward was standing in the book-room with the *Evening Mail* in his hand; you could almost have said that he looked excited. 'The Australians are here! They'll be practising at Lord's tomorrow.'

'And the summer,' said Jake, 'can be said to begin.

The Australians today, Mother tomorrow, perhaps the cuckoo the day after. And tonight Huck's little frolic. Such curious ideas children do have about the pleasures of picnics when everybody knows how very much more comfortable and convenient it is to eat one's meals indoors.'

All the same, Jake seemed to enjoy the evening as much as anybody. They had bought a huge assortment of food from the Chinese restaurant in Meadow Street. Everybody had chosen a favourite dish and Huck had insisted on adding fish and chips when they reached the Bar B. Quew farther up the road. Then they had walked to the playing fields up the canal, and on a patch of rough ground where the smooth turf became scrubland and then coppice, they had lit a fire and sprawled round it.

'I'm so full,' said Huck, dreamily licking her fingers, 'that I feel drunk. You can get drunk with food, I'm sure.' She looked at the range of school buildings at the top of the fields that stretched up on the other side of the canal. There was a light in one window. 'They've all gone home now. Perhaps that window's one poor boy who got left behind because he had measles or something. If it was term-time there would be lights everywhere because they would all be safely locked in. They would have done their compulsory hobbies, and now they would be drinking compulsory cocoa while a prefect told compulsory ghost stories.'

'You tell us a story,' said Jake, reclining on one elbow, 'instead of droning on like that.'

'You really want a story?' said Huck.

'Why not? In for a penny, in for a pound, I say. One might as well be hanged for a sheep as for a lamb; no sense in spoiling the ship for . . .'

'*You* stop droning.' Huck kicked him. 'I'll tell you the story of the Time Machine.'

'We've all read it,' said Jake with disgust, 'when we were kiddiwinks.'

'Not this one you haven't. You can't have, it's only just happened. Only people have got to listen and not interrupt.'

They did listen. Even Jake only muttered his facetious comments under his breath. It grew quite dark and they huddled round the ashes of the fire, trying to squeeze from it what remnants of warmth were left. A solitary star shone in the greeny-blue of the sky.

'And so,' Huck wound up, 'even Steve had his uses. He was like Gollum in *The Lord of the Rings*, you see. Gollum trailed around behind everybody until they wanted to murder him, because he was so taken up with the Ring (like Steve with the Time Machine), but it needed him to break the magic of the Ring. And it was the same with Steve. He's probably there now,' she pointed vaguely in the direction of the Meadow, 'looking for his Precious, like Barty said. Only he'll never find it, of course.'

There was a second or two of silence. 'Not at all bad, Huck, my dear little girl.' Jake nodded his head in a patriarchal way. 'I think we might even say that it showed promise.'

'It was quite cunning the way she grafted the fantasy bits on to what really did happen,' Polly conceded. 'I mean she made the bits about taking us all back into the past fit in fairly neatly with what we all have been doing. There were those ducks that one of Jake's mates gave him, and I did get all that material, and Sue has been reading out the family letters and stuff.'

'I like the touch about turning you into Mother's Great Aunt Mary,' Jake said. 'Poetic, that was. She was a frightful old harridan; I remember Granny talking about her. You'll be just the same – even when it comes to throwing things backwards instead of forwards.'

'Your sense of humour has always been warped,' said Polly coldly. 'Come on, we'd better be going. Pick up those plastic tubs, someone.'

But they lingered still. 'You look lost, Barty,' said Edward suddenly.

'Dreaming about computers,' said Jake.

Barty collected himself. 'I wasn't.'

'What, then? You were far enough away.'

'I was thinking,' said Barty, 'how nice Ned Huxtable was really, though we none of us liked him. He was so good and kind – but he didn't fit in, somehow; he wasn't in the right time.'

He didn't realize he had spoken aloud until he saw the others looking at him in astonishment.

'Why, Barty,' said Polly, 'you sound as though you had actually known him.'

Confused and embarrassed, he looked towards Huck.

'Of course he knew him. Haven't you been listening to anything I've been telling you? Come on, I want to get home, there's enough paint left for me to do another wall.'

'What a grasshopper mind that child has.' Jake scooped up a tub on the end of his shoe. 'One can't keep up with her ploys.'

'You know,' said Edward, nodding towards Barty. '*He's* the one that's changed.' He puzzled over it, kicking at the dead embers of the fire and tugging at his nose. 'Has he got a touch of Huck in him now, would you say?'

'Or perhaps,' said Jake, 'he's turned into Ned Huxtable's little brother. Which all goes to show, as my old grandad used to say, that you can't monkey around with Time Machines and expect to be the same afterwards.'

# When Hitler Stole Pink Rabbit

JUDITH KERR

Anna was only nine in 1933, too busy with her school work and her friends to take much notice of the posters of Adolf Hitler and the menacing swastikas plastered over Berlin. Being Jewish, she thought, was just something you were because your parents and grandparents were Jewish. Suddenly Anna's father was unaccountably and frighteningly missing. Shortly after, she and her brother were hurried out of Germany by their mother with alarming secrecy. Then began their rootless, wandering existence as refugees. Their life was often difficult and sad, but Anna soon discovered that all that really mattered was that the family was together.

An outstanding book for readers of ten upwards.

# Ballet Shoes for Anna

## NOEL STREATFEILD

When Anna and her two brothers are orphaned by an earth-
quake, which kills their parents and grandparents and totally
destroys their home, they leave Turkey and go to England to
live with their Uncle Cecil.

But after their carefree life in a caravan with their artist
father, it is difficult to adjust to living in a prim suburban
house with their stern uncle who disapproves of them and
opposes Anna's ambition to become a dancer. Her two
brothers, though, are determined that she continue her lessons
and set out to earn the money to pay for them.

'Humour and shrewdness go together in this expert story of
the dilemma of the children who feel their identities cramped
by unimaginative adults. It is Noel Streatfeild's gift to tell
a racy story and to mesh into it a wealth of technical detail.'

*Naomi Lewis*

*Thursday's Child* and the *Gemma* series by Noel Streatfeild are
also available in Lions.

# Harriet the Spy

## LOUISE FITZHUGH

Harriet the Spy has a secret notebook which she fills with utterly honest jottings about her parents, her friends and her neighbours. This, she feels sure, will prepare her for her career as a famous writer. Every day on her spy route, she scrutinizes, observes and notes down anything of interest to her:

> Laura Peters is thinner and uglier. I think she could do with some braces on her teeth.

> Once I thought I wanted to be Franca. But she's so dull if I was her I couldn't stand myself, I guess it's not money that makes people dull. I better find out because I might be it.

> If Marion Hawthorne doesn't watch out she's going to grow up into a lady Hitler.

But Harriet commits the unforgivable for a spy – she is unmasked. When her notebook is found by her school friends, their anger and retaliation and Harriet's unexpected responses explode in an hilarious and often touching way.

'Harriet M. Welsch is one of the meatiest heroines in modern juvenile literature. This novel is a *tour de force*.'

*Library Journal*

'This devastatingly shrewd, ruefully comic picture of the young makes a good many characters in children's fiction seem like wet dish-cloths.'

*Sunday Times*